TILLY AND ELMER'S
Carnal Calendar
TWELVE TALES OF FRISKY, RISKY, MISCHIEF

I0548862

TILLYANDELMER.COM

GENE CLEMENTS

Pickleworks Press
Sweet/Hot Editions

Acknowledgments

First of all, thanks to Tilly and Elmer, who seem to have camped out in my head. Usually they keep to themselves, but now and then they create a commotion that I have to look into and usually there's some kind of story behind the ruckus that I can't leave alone. I started writing about them several years ago and now they've more or less set up housekeeping in my imagination. Tilly especially is not someone who can be ignored for long and when she and Elmer began wrangling over what she'd like for Christmas, the die was cast – I had to start on *Tilly and Elmer's Carnal Calendar*.

I also have to give a nod of gratitude to my readers. When I began hanging out with Tilly and Elmer, my plan was only to find an amusing way to waste time, but after the original stories in *The Sexy Seniors of South Branch*, and *Coming of age in South Branch* were downloaded over fourteen thousand times, I began to think I might not be the only person who likes to waste time with them!

I'm always grateful to Ann who continues to encourage me, even when I miss my turn at cooking dinner, and who never fails to straighten me out when she notes that I've led Tilly and Elmer too far out of their ordinary extraordinary routines.

And, as usual, a profound "Thank You!" also goes to my editor, Elizabeth Johnson, who has gently saved me many times from blunders that I was pretending were brilliant writing!

~~~

CONTENTS

INTRODUCTION

These fictional tales record the amusing, playful, and sexy shenanigans of Tilly and Elmer, a Midwestern couple, now in their early seventies. They've been married for close to fifty years, they still really like each other, and they still know what to do about it!

To their occasional astonishment, they're no longer eighteen, but they often behave like mischievous eighteen-year-olds with a few exceptions like, you know, staying up all night, bending over without groaning, and having sex six times a day. What they've had to give up in quantity they've recouped in quality though, especially when there's a reason to celebrate! Of course, they have their little sexy traditions for major holidays – Valentine's Day, Fourth of July, Thanksgiving, and the like, but they don't forget to celebrate April Fool's Day, Mayday, and National Bourbon Day either! Now and then, they have to talk their way out of trouble or giggle at the minor scandals resulting from their indecorous comportment, but what would be the fun of living a scandal free lifestyle anyway?

Tilly and Elmer live on a farm five miles west of the made-up town of South Branch, Iowa. They were high school sweethearts in South Branch over fifty years ago, and now that they've both retired, they spend their time attempting to recapture their long-ago youth - or resting up from the effort.

PROLOGUE

"Wait 'till you hear this, Lance!" Tilly said. "We'll have to think up a new way to celebrate!"

"Tilly, did you just call me 'Lance'?" Elmer asked.

"Yes, I did! And you can call me 'Lulu'! It's national 'Get a Different Name Day'!"

"It's WHAT?"

"National 'Get a Different Name Day'! You can go back to 'Elmer' tomorrow if you want to, but I propose we celebrate this major holiday by jumping into bed and you can make me scream 'Oh YES, Lance, keep doing it just like that!' "

"Tilly, I wouldn't mind spending the afternoon in bed with you, and 'Lance and Lulu' has a nice ring to it, but if I were to get used to calling you 'Lulu', it could turn out to be troublesome later. And if you start screaming 'OH YES LANCE BABY! You're the BEST!' I might get out of bed and start looking in the closet for this guy!"

"If you're going to be grumpy about 'Different Name Day', I guess we could put that idea on hold for three days."

"Why three days?"

"Well, you might be more in the mood three days from now when I could celebrate 'Do a Grouch a Favor Day' with you!"

~~~

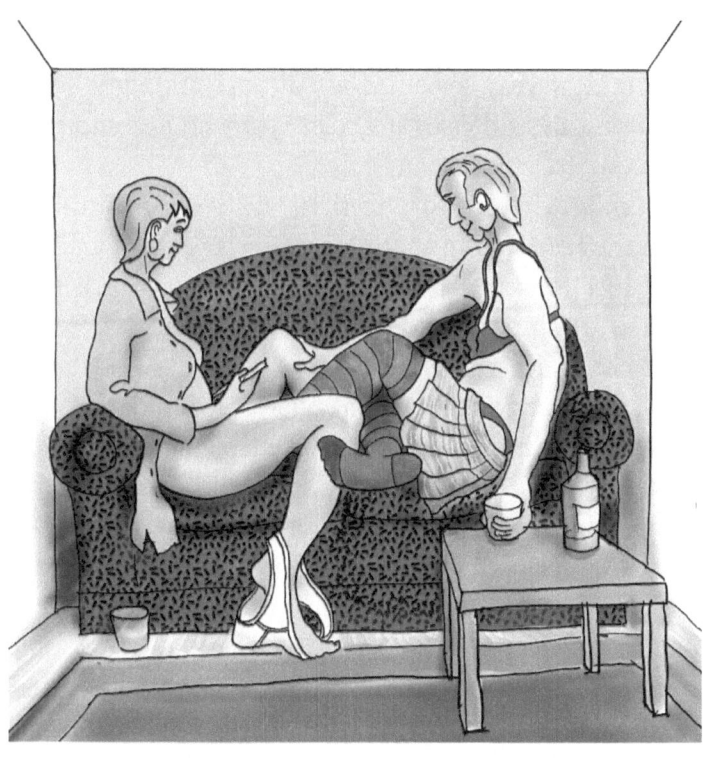

1

TILLY AND ELMER'S UNRULY RESOLUTIONS

Tilly snuggled up next to her husband and tickled him awake. "Good morning and happy New Year's Eve, Elmer!"

"How did New Year's Eve get here so early?" he mumbled.

"Come on 'Wiggle Bear!', it's the last day of the year

and you know what that means!"

"Of course I do, Tilly! But we don't usually start having new year sex until it's almost midnight so we can bring the old year to a celebratory climax and greet the new year with a bang!"

"I'm looking forward to that!" Tilly said. "But don't forget to be thinking about New Year's resolutions first. And just for fun, I think you should make MY New Year's Resolutions and I should make yours this year for a change!"

"That sounds perilous but hilarious!" Elmer mused.

Tilly and Elmer had discovered some decades ago that any New Year's resolutions they made had a remarkably low likelihood of being successfully carried out, even (or perhaps especially) if their intended plans were wise and healthy. This led to mild feelings of guilt and so they shifted their thinking regarding declarations demanding desirable behavior; they decided to make a game out of inventing the most unlikely, frivolous, and impossible New Year's resolutions they could think of, so that a failure to follow through might often be a good idea.

After supper, in the company of a bottle of Bourbon, they retired to the small, cozy room in the attic of their century old farmhouse five miles west of South Branch, IA. This tiny room was enclosed primarily with old bookcases, unused keepsakes and knickknacks, and boxes containing unknown but possibly precious objects from the distant past. The accommodations featured a well-used but still comfortable love seat which had survived the more athletic sexual adventures of their younger days, a profusion of pillows, a basket of blankets, and a small coffee table. A large window in the gable end of the room looked out over the moonlit fields and woods south of the house. An armoire containing a varied assortment of old clothing flanked the narrow doorway. The contents could be used for dressing up in, ripping off each other, or as towels for wiping splattered liquids from surfaces.

They began their annual sojourn into the world of plots they never expected to carry out by toasting the end of another year together with a glass of their favorite libation. This was accompanied by trying on various articles of clothing to ascertain which look would most suit the topic of their get-together. Tilly proposed that, in keeping with the idea that each would be making up unacceptable New Year's resolutions for the other, they should dress in each other's clothing as a means of inspiration. After some trial and error, Tilly decided on one of Elmer's long dress shirts worn above an old pair of Elmer's white Y front briefs that had long ago paid their debt to society. On Tilly's advice, Elmer squeezed his body into a lacy red bra and matching panties that he had loved when they fit Tilly thirty years ago, topped by a plaid, pleated miniskirt from the nineteen seventies and striped knee-high socks. Each looked ridiculous, but that problem diminished as they sipped a second glass of Bourbon.

"Ok, ladies first Elmer! And since you're dressed as

a woman, we'll start with my first New Year's resolution for you! Next year you resolve to get us thrown into jail for public indecency!"

"That one will be hard for me to keep, Tilly. You know I get kind of shy about that kind of thing. Of course, I suppose you might get me drunk and force me to do it! You have been known to secretly enjoy exhibitionism although I doubt you'd like being in jail that much!"

"Oh Elmer, I'm sure a clever boy like you will find a way to protect his demure and innocent wife from any unpleasantness like that!"

"I appreciate your overconfidence in me! Are you going to write these down, Tilly, just so we don't forget any of them?"

"I always write them down to be sure our memory isn't obscured later by our refreshments!"

"Good. Are you ready for the first resolution I've made for you, Tilly?"

"Sure, why not?"

"You resolve to take up your true calling next year and become a dominatrix! Any man who fails to carry out your demands at once will be severely punished!"

"I'm sure that won't happen Elmer; where on earth would I find a man who wouldn't already do exactly as I say at all times?"

"I know you'll have a hard time trying to keep that resolution, Tilly. Especially since you're too nice and sweet to ever take a man out to the barn, tie him up naked in the hay loft, and spank him with a riding crop over some minor misdemeanor!"

"You know I would never even think of such a thing!" Tilly said, as she thought about how it might be a good idea to apply a dose of corrective impact to the bottom of her occasionally imperfect husband now and then.

"All right Elmer, here's your next resolution! You resolve to become world famous on the internet for some kind of naughty behavior. And just for the record, it had better involve me and not some OTHER oversexed girl! Otherwise, I might have to keep my resolution to tie you up naked and spank you in the hay loft!"

"It might be fun to become a scandalous international celebrity Tilly, but I seriously doubt I could think of anything that would bring that about. I think I can safely say I won't be keeping that resolution!"

"I'm sure you'll want to keep the next resolution I have for YOU though Tilly! It's likely that at some time during the year a bevy of attractive women will finally realize that I'm the handsomest and most charming man in South Branch and will begin fighting over which of them will be the recipient of my favors. Naturally, I'll try to resist them, but I could be powerless to repel their attentions and you might be called on to save me from their overzealous affections. Just think of how terrible it would be if your loving husband were to be overpowered by such a desperate mob of lovesick ladies!"

"Ok, Elmer, I may be able to step in. It's possible though, that I'll be busy down at Claire's Hair Affair just when you need my help. But luckily, since I was a nurse, I can tape any of your body parts back together, if I can find any, once they've had their way with you."

"You might WANT to keep my next resolution for you, though Elmer! This one could make us a fortune if you don't break it!"

"A fortune you say? I might just resolve to keep this one, Tilly. What is it?"

"You know we go to the county fair every summer and that our favorite thing is to take a ride on the Ferris Wheel, right?"

"Yes."

"And it's our little tradition that I pull up my skirt and slip my panties off when we get to the top, right!"

"That's my favorite sideshow, yes!"

"But I always pull my skirt down when we get near the ground so my little trick isn't that obvious to people who aren't looking carefully, right?"

"Yes. That's a good idea in my opinion."

"Well, if you were to set up a little viewing area next to the Ferris Wheel, you could sell tickets to dirty old men and I could forget to pull my skirt down when I pass close by on every revolution. I want you to resolve to earn a few bucks that way next summer!"

"It will take a lot of takers for us to earn a fortune at

a nickel a ticket, Tilly!"

"Are you kidding Elmer? Men would pay a grand a glance for a gander at my glorious girly bits!"

"Hmmm. I'll definitely give that a lot of thought, Tilly!"

As if to evaluate Tilly's idea, Elmer reached under the shirttail that covered her thighs and began to remove the men's briefs covering the private parts she proposed to present for public viewing.

"That will cost you a thousand, Elmer!" she said grandly.

"How about another glass of Bourbon instead?"

"Ok."

They took a brief break from their game, sipping their drinks while Elmer studied Tilly's lady parts. Judging from the portions of his genitalia that began squeezing out from the edges of Elmer's too small panties, he seemed to feel that the view between Tilly's legs might actually be worth a thousand bucks at that.

"I'll take your 'I see London, I see France, I see Tilly's lost her underpants!' idea under advisement, Tilly. In the meantime here's my next resolution for you: 'I, Tilly, resolve to have a frisky fling with a female friend this year'!"

"What! That's not going to happen Elmer! Don't be silly! Me having some kind of sexual shenanigans with a woman? You know I would never consider anything like that."

"Just as I thought. You're protesting too much my

dear. It's probably your greatest fantasy!"

"It's NOT my greatest fantasy! It's at least second or third!"

"Don't forget, you've told me about some of your college adventures, Tilly!"

"Well, nothing really happened, and anyway, I was young at the time. And we didn't do anything THAT unusual. Not in nineteen-sixties San Francisco anyway. I probably wouldn't even be tempted nowadays. At least not very tempted. And anyway, I won't have any trouble breaking that resolution since I don't know of any candidates for my secret affections. Except you, when you're wearing that cute miniskirt of course!"

"Well, write it down anyway just in case an old girlfriend comes to town or something."

"Here's one for you that's not so far-fetched, Elmer. You might even be able to keep this resolution since we've done it before. This year you resolve to park in a semi risky location some evening after dark and make love to me in the pickup!"

"Hmmm. It's true we used to do that when we were so hot for each other we didn't pay any attention to the risk, but at this point I have a little hesitation about becoming the center of South Branch gossip. Not only that, but you may remember that the last time we tried doing it in the truck I threw my back out!"

"So you're predicting that you'll break even this easy and pleasant resolution?"

"I'll try to make it up to you somehow, Tilly!"

"Aren't you worried that if you break this resolution someone will find my vibrator and me alone together in the truck some night? Talk about gossip!"

"I'll have to keep a close watch on you. There's no doubt about it!"

"That would probably be wise, Elmer!"

"Okay, here's your next one, Tilly, which I'm sure you'll want to keep. You resolve to let me anoint your beautiful naked body with thick fluid and then roll around on the floor with me and get it all over us."

"What kind of thick fluid, Elmer?"

"Something perfectly safe so we can lick it off each other!"

"If you're planning for us to lick it off each other, it had better be whipped cream, Elmer!"

"Whipped cream? Well that would be one idea, Tilly!"

"Okay! Here's my last resolution for you, Elmer. Are you ready for the grand finale? I'm going to insist that you keep this resolution big boy!"

"I'm ready!"

"I can SEE THAT by the bulge in your panties! And, it's almost midnight already! Starting right now you resolve to snuggle under the covers with me on this old love seat and show me how a man in a sexy miniskirt treats a girl with nothing on but his old shirt!"

"Be it so resolved, Tilly! Just the resolution we need for bringing the old year to a proper climax and welcoming the new one with frisky fireworks!"

~~~

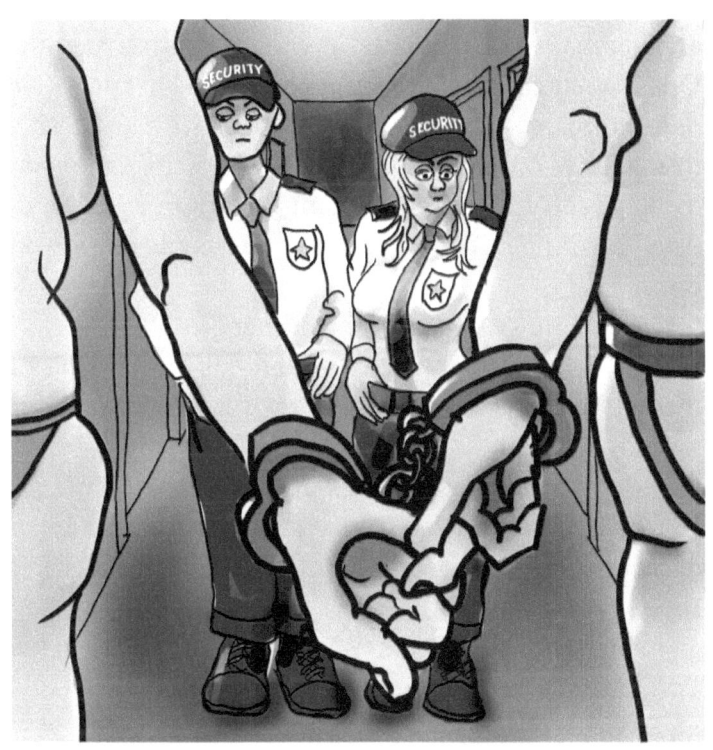

2
VALENTINE MONKEYSHINES

"All right, Elmer!" Tilly said in the tone of voice she always used when there was a serious discussion coming.

Elmer warily looked up from his newspaper. "All right WHAT?"

"It's February 12th!"

"Oh! Of course."

He searched his memory: Her birthday? No. Their

anniversary? No, that was in the summer sometime. One of their children's or grandchildren's birthdays? He didn't think so. The blank look on his face caused Tilly to take pity on him; after all, the ability to remember dates wasn't the only important quality in a husband. And Valentine's Day was coming; she should go easy on him.

"Valentine's Day is coming, Elmer!"

"Oh, right! I guess we've gotten out of the habit of making a big deal out of it after forty-nine years of marriage."

"We're making a big deal out of it this year, Wiggle Bear!" Tilly said, using a nickname she had made-up decades ago right after they had made love for the first time.

"You haven't called me 'Wiggle Bear' for thirty years. You must have something special planned!"

"We're going to plan it together, but I expect we'll both be bare and wiggly before we're finished!"

"Ok, Flash, where do we start?" he said, using his old pet name for her.

"I want to do something scandalous! That means we'll have to go far away from South Branch or people will be gossiping about us like they did after we went to Las Vegas that time!"

"As I recall, Tilly, you weren't fond of THAT scandal when we got a little drunk and did it in the window of our hotel. Especially when the police photos turned up on the front page of the South Branch Sentinel!"

"That adventure gives me a little thrill when I think

back on it now. We're too straight laced, Elmer! I want to do something dirty and kinky and shocking! Maybe we could go to a peep show or something!"

"Well, that's not the most shocking thing I can think of although it does sound like fun for ME. But Tilly, I'm not sure you'd ..."

"I hear they have peep shows where the strippers are men!" Tilly said as though she had studied up on the subject.

"Male strippers? I don't know Tilly. What if everyone in the place begged me to hop up on the stage and strip down and as soon as I walked in?"

"If they do Elmer, I'll put the first twenty in your jock strap!"

Apart from a bit of hesitation about taking Tilly to a club where the men were performing partly naked (he hoped it was only partly), Elmer was enthusiastic about the idea, and booked an expensive room at a fancy hotel in St. Louis. Tilly added to his enthusiasm when she announced that, to lighten the weight of their suitcase, she intended to leave all her panties at home. This made the four-hour drive to St. Louis especially entertaining and by the time they got there, they felt more like eighteen year olds than they had since they were eighteen.

The first order of business, after reluctantly deciding that they shouldn't wear themselves out in bed before looking up the nearest lingerie and/or sex toy shop, was to look up the nearest lingerie and/or sex toy shop. Tilly and Elmer rarely had the opportunity to visit these kinds of places, there were none within fifty miles of South Branch, and after an hour of shocking shopping, they had selected a hope chest worth of naughty baubles. Among other unmentionables, Elmer insisted on buying Tilly a pair of crotchless panties, and Tilly found him a cute pair of silky men's underwear that featured a completely open backside and only a small net hammock below a large, centrally placed opening in the front, which would allow his member to escape from any unwelcome confinement. These formed the underpinnings of their evening's attire and, over drinks and dinner at the hotel, they decided to try out the strip club that Tilly had recommended after a thorough on-line search.

They took a taxi to the club, which was, of course, garish, sleazy, and freakishly illuminated with pink and blue lights, just as Tilly had hoped. She and Elmer were greeted with good cheer and were seated at a small table near the stage. The music was loud and the waitress, who was clad exclusively in tight red vinyl shorts and platform shoes, gave Elmer a bit of a boost when she playfully squeezed his shoulder and gave him a close up view of her breasts as she reached across the table with Tilly's drink. Elmer began massaging Tilly's thigh just under her skirt.

After a time the house lights were dimmed and spotlights focused on a remarkably muscular, handsome, and protuberant young man on the stage. He was dressed in tight clothing meant to suggest a uniform, and this he removed item by item during his gyrations until he was completely naked. Elmer found this a bit more risqué than necessary, but he was just inebriated enough to take Tilly at her word when she leaned close to him and shouted over the music, "He looks just like you, Elmer!"

Tilly and Elmer were having fun, and as the evening progressed with more drinks, more bare bodies, and more flirtatious fondling from the staff and each other, they were in unspoken agreement that this was the sexiest Valentine's Day they had enjoyed together in decades. As much fun as they were having however, they were aware that they were not, in fact, eighteen any longer and if they wanted to get back to the hotel with enough energy for their planned night of wild sex, they had better not stay too long.

The combination of low inhibitions and high arousal made the cab ride back to the hotel thrilling, and no doubt gave the cabbie a story to tell about the horny old people that almost did it in the back seat of his cab. The frisky foolishness of the evening led to a series of increasingly outrageous whispered, but vetoed, dares between them, regarding how much clothing they were willing to remove before entering the hotel lobby.

Once back in their private hideaway, the foreplay continued with a champagne toast, inept dancing, and clumsy removal of each other's garments until both were naked except for their skimpy new underclothes. Tilly's lady parts were framed in all their smooth-shaven splendor within the wide-open crotch of her panties, and Elmer's now abundantly interested manhood was fully on display as it ascended from the opening above the tiny net cradling his testicles. Laughter and teasing ensued. This led to a return of the dare vs. dare they had begun in the cab and, with a laugh, Tilly dared Elmer to walk out into the corridor in his current attire. Given the sorry state of his sobriety, and his full tank of testosterone, Elmer didn't see why it wouldn't be quite safe to dash out into the public hallway for a second. It was late and the odds of someone returning to a nearby room at that moment were low. Besides, he could check to be sure the coast was clear before beginning his mischievous mission.

"If I do it, you have to do it next!" he told her.

"If you do it, I'll stay out there twice as long!" Tilly promised.

Elmer cautiously opened the door to the hallway and looked around. He didn't see anyone and couldn't hear any noise from the nearby elevator so he stepped fully out and did a twirl in the middle of the hall, then hastened back into the room.

"Your turn," he said to Tilly.

With a giggle, Tilly boldly stepped into the middle of the hallway and did the best she could to attempt a belly dance while Elmer watched from the open door. The hallway remained empty and nothing embarrassing had happened thus far so Tilly and Elmer became more daring in their eccentric exploits. Each took additional turns nearly naked in the hallway and each turn featured a longer, clumsier, and more hilarious, attempt at dancing. Over the course of perhaps ten minutes Tilly and Elmer became so amused by each other's entertaining gyrations in the corridor as they watched from the doorway that they almost forgot that these shenanigans were being carried out in a public space. This inattention was about to cause an incident.

Tilly decided to attempt a drunken demonstration of the motion of twirling a hula-hoop around her waist and in the process, as her breasts went one direction and her bottom went the other, she toppled over. She clearly wasn't hurt, but Elmer naturally went out to help her up and as he did so, the door to their room closed with a very solid sounding "tick-SHLUMPT!"

Neither Tilly nor Elmer recognized the extent of their problem at first, but their lethargic thought processes eventually made them aware that they were locked out of their room in clothing that was probably even more scandalous than ordinary nudity. This was annoyingly sobering, but still worth a few snickers. The only thing they could think of was to send one of them down to the front desk to ask for a replacement keycard, but neither was eager to make the trip. One idea was to let Elmer cover the exposed centerpiece of his genitalia with what little there was of Tilly's panties and approach the front desk as though he dressed that way all the time. Tilly pointed out that this would leave her totally naked there in the hallway, just as the police were probably downstairs hauling him away. As Elmer considered the merits of her argument, they heard the elevator stop at their floor.

A uniformed man and woman exited the elevator and began walking toward them briskly.

"See you in jail!" Tilly whispered, hoping she was joking.

"What's going on?" the man asked unsmilingly. Tilly and Elmer suppressed giggles since the "Security Guards" looked to them like they were about twelve years old.

"I'm sorry officer," Elmer said. "We've gotten locked out of our room."

"It's unlawful in this state to appear without clothing in a public place," the officer responded sternly.

"Well, we aren't completely naked," Elmer pointed out, then wished he hadn't.

The officer began fondling a pair of handcuffs attached to his belt. "I'll need to see your identification!"

Elmer thought it should have been obvious that if he had any identification on him it would have to be hidden in a place the officer wouldn't want to look into. "It's locked in the room."

"We're not authorized to give anyone access to a guestroom without positive identification," the officer said, as though this would settle the matter.

Tilly smiled at the man's attempt to impress his young female partner by exhibiting inflated courage in apprehending a naked old couple.

As the officer reached for the two-way radio at his belt, two women, about Tilly and Elmer's age, emerged from the elevator, embracing and kissing each other as though they might not make it all the way to their room before their desire for one another exploded into a sexual frenzy right there in the hallway. On discovering the commotion already underway outside their door, the couple looked at Tilly and Elmer carefully.

"Tilly?" said the thinner of the two women.

"Claire! What a surprise! Elmer, this is Claire, my hairdresser. And you know Mary Ann, South Branch's most experienced librarian."

Although hugs would have been customary, the foursome skipped them on this occasion. Tilly hadn't known that Claire and Mary Ann were involved in a lesbian relationship; this surprised her somewhat because Mary Ann was married and was also carrying on a not very secret affair with the mayor of South Branch and Claire had an occasional boyfriend from Mount Pleasant. The outnumbered security force was forgotten, as the unplanned nature of their meeting became the topic of an extended conversation among the South Branch delegation.

"How come you're almost naked out in the hallway?" Claire finally got around to asking.

"We locked ourselves out accidentally," Tilly told her.

"Come on into our room! We'll loan Elmer one of the hotel bathrobes and he can go down and get a key while we catch up!" Claire turned away from the officers and lowered her voice. "It goes without saying that none of us should recount the details of this coincidence once we get back to South Branch, right?"

"What happens in St. Louis stays in St. Louis!" Tilly laughed.

Claire opened the door to their room and the

foursome went inside, leaving the security patrol alone in the hallway.

The brave security staff looked in each other's eyes and then set out toward the elevator, thankful for the opportunity to turn their attention to other affairs.

~~~

3
APRIL FOOLISHNESS

The bedside clock read 2 AM, and Elmer was awake considering how to outdo Tilly tomorrow in their usual unspoken April Fool's Day test of trickiness. He got up to use the bathroom, and on his way back to bed, he had the big idea – he would swap the location of his and Tilly's underwear drawers in the dresser!

"This will be a good one!" Elmer thought to himself, silently removing and rearranging the drawer locations.

Their custom was to engage in a bit of friendly foolishness on April Fool's day, and Elmer was sure this would fool Tilly when she first got up, before she had even had time to set a trap for him. As it turned out, he was right; when she got out of the shower the next morning, Tilly opened her underwear drawer, only to find a cluttered mess of random underclothing instead of her ordinary orderly organization of undies. It only took her a moment however, to realize that the untidy assortment of underpants arrayed before her belonged to her husband.

"Elmer, what have you done with my panties?" she asked.

Elmer giggled. "What do you mean?" he asked innocently.

"Oh never mind, here they are!" she announced. Elmer had expected his trick to have a little more impact, but he supposed it WAS kind of obvious. The morning passed without further trickery, and Elmer began to think his wife had forgotten to outsmart him with a humiliating hoax this year.

Tilly was going to have lunch with her friends in town and Elmer looked forward to spending the afternoon privately perusing pornography on the Internet. Of course Tilly was generally aware that he sometimes indulged in this common husbandly hobby, but he didn't really want her studying his deviant downloads in any detail. Elmer had, over time, built up a naughty little collection of kinky videos involving mature women in their underwear, spanking naked older men as though they were misbehaving schoolboys. He thought any discovery of this tiny, harmless stash of trash might cause Tilly to look askance at his perfectly proper, yet peculiar practice, and so he had taken at least modest measures to keep it hidden. As to his little fetish, Elmer was uncertain as to whether he would enjoy actually receiving this sort of thrashing himself, but he definitely found the idea a turn on.

Toward late afternoon, Elmer heard the back door slam and quickly closed his laptop before Tilly came into the living room.

"How was lunch?" he asked.

"Great! Wait until you hear this Elmer! I might be writing for the South Branch Sentinel!"

"What brought this about?" Elmer asked, having never pictured Tilly as a writer.

"Well, you know my friend Linda writes for the Sentinel, and she told me at lunch that the woman who writes the "Ask Mrs. Milfton", sex advice column, is going to move to Barbados with a young trucker she just met at Rosalie's Palm! So – they need someone to take her place!"

"You're going to write a sex advice column in the local newspaper?"

This gave Elmer pause! He could just picture his friends at Pearl's Downtown Diner giving him a hard time over everything she wrote.

"Sure, why not?"

"Well, for one thing, you don't know anything about

the subject!"

Elmer knew this didn't come out the way it should have.

"I mean of course you know about sex, but you don't know all the medical and psychological stuff!"

"You may have forgotten I was a nurse, Elmer! Not to mention the fact that I had to teach YOU everything about it!"

Tilly had lived in San Francisco during the "Summer of Love" so she was probably right, and Elmer knew better than to continue in this vein, anyway.

"I'm sure you'll be great at it," he said, trying to sound enthusiastic. "When do you start?"

"It isn't a done deal quite yet. I have some sample letters to "Mrs. Milfton" that I have to write responses to. They want to see how I do on them before they hire me, but I think it looks good. Linda introduced me to the editor and she'll put in a good word for me."

"Are they real letters?"

"Of course they're 'real' letters, Elmer! Real in the sense that someone wrote them, anyway. This is a small town and although there are plenty of kinky people around, most people won't send their questions to the newspaper because they're afraid their neighbors will recognize them! You are sworn to secrecy about this though, Elmer!"

"All right. So who DOES write the letters?"

"Well, some DO come from confused citizens of South Branch, but most of them come from others who work at the paper. They go out drinking Friday nights and then amuse themselves by writing letters to the sex columnist. I think the editor picks the ones they will print and the best ones get a little prize of some kind. I'm planning to call my column 'Tell it to Tilly'. You can help me with the responses to these sample letters Elmer. It will be fun, want to try some?"

"I guess so."

"Ok, here's the first one:
'Dear Mrs. Milfton,
My wife and I are in our mid sixties and, for some reason, she wants to have sex all the time! It was fun when we were young, but we're not teenagers any more and I think we're too old for such foolishness. Besides, her constant complaining about it interferes with my drinking! How can I get her to stop pestering me?
Signed: Tired Hubby''

What do you think, Elmer?"

"I think you should give her my email address!" Elmer said before giving the matter the proper amount of thought.

"Very funny, Elmer," Tilly said solemnly.

"Ok, how about suggesting she find a younger man to amuse herself with while the old man is passed out?" Elmer offered.

"That's probably good advice, but this is a family paper and South Branch is too conservative for that response. I don't want to get reams of complaints every time I put out a column! How about: 'This isn't her problem, it's yours! Perhaps you should spend some time thinking back to what you did at eighteen and then take her out to your old parking spot in the country. It might be more fun than the bottle, and better for your health!' "

Elmer thought for a minute. "Maybe you should also throw in something about perking up his pecker with some Internet porn!"

"I don't think my readers would appreciate that suggestion, but I'm glad to hear you're an expert on Internet porn, Elmer!"

"Well, my friends tell me there's plenty out there, that's all," Elmer said, telling part of the truth.

"All right, let's try another one:
'Dear Mrs. Milfton,
My husband keeps dressing up in my underwear! He even switched our dresser drawers so that he could get into my panties easier! What's a girl to do?
Signed: Running low on knickers.' "

Elmer looked at Tilly suspiciously. "I wasn't wearing your underwear this morning, I was just teasing you on April Fools' Day by switching the drawers."

"I know that Elmer, but maybe lots of husbands think they look good in pink silk panties!"

"Maybe," Elmer said.

"How about if I tell her to just keep buying more panties until her husband gets tired of funding her shopping sprees?" Tilly proposed.

"Maybe he should buy his own ladies' panties," Elmer suggested.

"I think most of my readers would prefer it if I suggest it isn't OK for a man to go around wearing ladies' underwear all the time. Maybe she should padlock her underwear drawer. Or she could take a picture of him and threaten to send it to his pals."

Elmer offered another idea. "She could start wearing his underpants. Or take up the habit of not wearing any panties and then throwing all of hers away!"

"I like your last idea, no panties in the house at all. I doubt it would satisfy my readers though. Maybe she could spank him whenever she catches him wearing her underwear," Tilly chuckled.

Elmer found this suggestion a little bit exciting.

"I'll go along with that idea! Are there any more letters?" Elmer said.

"Here's the last one:

"Dear Mrs. Milfton,

I suppose all men like to look at dirty pictures on the Internet now and then. But I've just discovered that my husband seems to be unnaturally interested in pictures or videos of mature women spanking naked men! I could understand it if the women he liked to look at were young, skinny women wearing high heels and black leather! That would be quite normal. But he likes the ones where an older, matronly woman is spanking a completely naked older man. I think this is perverted and I can't figure out how to deal with it. And, I can never find a good time to confront him about it because he's always busy cooking my dinner, taking out the trash, or vacuuming the living room. Am I just being a prude about this?

Signed: Too nice to him."

Elmer was taken aback. The letter described his own harmless fetish perfectly, and it didn't seem like a coincidence, even though he thought his private stash was sufficiently hidden from a casual visitor to his computer. In spite of his suspicions, he decided to go along with the discussion, lest he admit to something Tilly didn't already know about.

"That doesn't seem like a big deal to me," Elmer said, trying not to sound defensive. "Just tell her to mind her own business!"

"It sounds shocking to me, Elmer!" Tilly said. "Why would he get off on fantasizing about being spanked by an old woman? It's perverted!"

"Maybe he wouldn't want it to actually happen. It could be that the idea just turns him on for some reason," Elmer said.

"But maybe he really does want to be spanked by a strange woman. That sounds like what he wants to me. What if it leads to him finding someone who will fulfill his fantasy, while his wife is sitting home alone, wondering where he is! What if that happens?"

"If that happens she might have to fix her own supper, the lazy bitch!" Elmer said, and then wished he hadn't.

"Let's not make her the culprit here, Elmer! He's

very close to crossing the line in my opinion!"

"Crossing WHAT line?" Elmer said crossly.

"The line of being over the line! If he wanted look at pictures of a man wearing a dog collar around his neck and some sexy lady in a leather bra, short shorts, and nine-inch heels parading him around her apartment on a leash that would be fine. It wouldn't be realistic to think he might actually be doing this because he'd have to go to St. Louis or Chicago to find someone like that. But any older woman in South Branch would jump at the opportunity to take a man home, make him get naked, then strip down to a dirty bra and panties and spank him until he couldn't sit down for a week. Lots of women around here think all men deserve that kind of treatment anyway! In fact, I'd say he has probably indulged in this debauchery many times already if he's collecting reminders of his depravity on his computer. The scoundrel!"

"That's crazy!" said Elmer.

"You're right, he IS crazy!" Tilly responded.

Making sure she couldn't see the screen, Elmer opened his laptop and closed the folder he had been looking at when she came in.

"What WOULD YOU advise her to do then?" Elmer said with some hesitation.

"Well, I'd advise her to punish him severely of course!" Tilly said.

"And how is she going to do that?" Elmer demanded.

"Take off your clothes and I'll show you, Elmer!"

Tilly said, beginning to unbutton her blouse.

"WHAT?"

Tilly demonstrated on Elmer how an older woman should punish a man who was guilty of such decadence. As it turned out, Elmer actually DID like being spanked by an older woman in real life just as much as he liked looking at pictures of that activity.

Elmer recovered after a few minutes, although he chose not to sit down.

"So, are you going to put THAT suggestion in your column?"

"What column?"

"Your sex advice column of course, 'Tell it to Tilly'?"

"Oh, that!" she said.

"Yes, that! So what are you going to say?"

"How about 'APRIL FOOL'?"

~~~

4

HOORAY, HOORAY, THE FIRST OF MAY

Elmer's custom was to drive into South Branch most mornings and have coffee at Pearl's Downtown Diner with his buddies Al, Tex, and Virgil.

"Good morning, gentlemen," Elmer said. "And I'm using that word loosely! Have I missed massive merriment this morning?"

"Hey Elmer! Nope. Nothing but a blow by blow description of what Al and Wanda used to do in the front seat of his Dodge Dart back fifty years ago."

"Well, I've overheard that overstated oration a hundred times, so I guess I won't miss missing it this time."

The daily discussion normally varied within a narrow range of topics including the weather, the hotness of their former high school girlfriends, the superiority of old cars that you could repair yourself, and the preeminence of their favorite sports teams as compared to their companion's favorites.

"Happy May first, by the way," Elmer said.

"It IS the first of May, Isn't it?" Al said. "That reminds me of an old saying, 'Hooray, hooray, the first of May...' "

The others responded in unison. *"Outdoor fucking starts today!"*, Keeping their voices down so as not to incur the wrath of Pearl, who disapproved of profanity, even if it WAS coming from the old regulars.

"That brings back memories!" said Al.

"Right, memories of what Wanda wouldn't let you get away with!" Tex reminded him.

"How were the boys at Pearl's?" Tilly asked when Elmer got home.

"Does the phrase 'Hooray, hooray, the first of May...' sound familiar?" he asked.

"You ask me that every year Elmer, and then you tell me the rest of the jingle."

"Well, today IS the first of May!" Elmer said hopefully.

"And it IS remarkably nice outside. I wouldn't mind a little caper in the clover this afternoon," Tilly said. "I'm pretty sure that's why you brought this up."

"You know me too well," Elmer said. "I feel the call of the wild on a day like this!"

After lunch, Tilly and Elmer gathered up some blankets, their favorite lube, Tilly's trusty toy just in case, and a bottle of wine, and then set off out the back door, heading for the wide spot in the creek about a half-mile away. They walked along the edge of the field and then took the path through the woods. This had been their favorite skinny-dipping spot years ago, but some houses had been built nearby in recent years and it was no longer as private as they were looking for. A few hundred yards beyond their old spot however, the woods extended farther from the creek, and they found a perfect grassy location at the edge of a field where it met the trees. It was a warm afternoon and several large oaks provided protection and dappled shade.

Unlike their younger days, they were in no hurry. They carefully arranged the blankets to provide proper padding and then opened the wine. By way of easing into the frolic, they took their shoes off, Tilly removed her top and bra, and Elmer took off his shirt. They sipped wine, recalled earlier open-air erotic escapades, and relaxed into the rhythm of the afternoon. Before long the wine, the sensation of early summer, the warm breeze, the sexy feeling of being naked outdoors, and the inner sense of naughtiness, conspired to make them completely captivated. They began to imagine themselves as wild animals, inhabiting the woods and behaving completely in accordance with their natural proclivities. As they sat tranquilly touching each other, the woodland creatures seemed to accept them as neighbors; rabbits and squirrels resumed their hopping and scampering in the underbrush, birds called to each other in the treetops, and a bald eagle even soared across the field to land in a nearby tree.

"I feel like we've become a part of nature," Tilly said. "Let's do something natural!"

"Like what?" Elmer inquired. "I thought what we came here to do was perfectly natural!"

"I don't know. Something like a wild animal would do. I know, let's do a mating dance of some kind?"

Elmer thought about this and then poured another glass of wine. "I think sipping wine is the natural mating dance of the species called Homo sapiens," he proclaimed.

"The wine is a good beginning," Tilly said, "but come on Elmer, take those pants off and dance naked with me like we're wild animals! Don't be shy, no one can see us out here!"

The bottle was finished before they felt fully feral, but this did lead to an impromptu and inelegant but hilarious dance in the grass around the blanket. Their bizarre behavior somewhat resembled a chase, with Elmer stumbling after Tilly and then, when he stopped to rest, Tilly turning to chase him. After a few turns around their nest, they tumbled into a heap on the blanket and began a remarkably energetic session of entangled squirming together involving simultaneous kissing of far flung body parts. After a while, Tilly retrieved the lube from their supplies, applied a generous dollop where necessary, and the lovers rearranged themselves into the traditional position for sexual intercourse among Homo sapiens. A naturalist would report that their movements were less frenzied but ultimately just as focused as the mating habits of younger members of the species.

As it turned out, a naturalist did report exactly this to his colleagues as they watched the "Eagle Cam" positioned to provide 24/7 monitoring of an eagle's nest in one of the trees above Tilly and Elmer's aerie. This camera was one of many positioned to record the activity in eagle's nests across the country, and the video feed from this cam was streamed live to bird watchers around the world. As it happened, the camera recorded a slightly wider frame than just the nest itself and Tilly and Elmer's love nest below was included in this field of view. As the pair began their courtship display, exactly 291 people across the globe were no longer focusing their attention on fledgling eagles but on the pre coital cuddling of Homo sapiens. Word travels fast on the Internet, and by the time Elmer began using his undershirt to dry the fluids that had collected on their skin, 2714 were watching.

Tilly and Elmer knew that one or two eagle's nests in northern Iowa could be viewed on line, but they had no idea that such a thing was going on in the woods south of South Branch. They were, however, about to become aware of that awkward information.

The next morning, when he arrived at Pearl's, Elmer was surprised to be greeted with a standing ovation from his pals and several other denizens of South Branch.

"So, you've all finally realized what a magnificent example of upstanding manhood I am, have you!" Elmer said with a laugh.

"Well, you were magnificent yesterday afternoon anyway!" Al said. "How did you know that camera was there?"

"Camera?" Elmer said.

"Don't try to tell us you chose exactly that spot by accident!"

"Chose what spot?" Elmer said, beginning to worry a little that someone had seen the two of them in the woods.

"That spot where you and Tilly were, um, 'mating', out in the woods! You're famous now, and not just in South Branch!"

"What are you talking about?" Elmer said, confused and a little concerned.

"The video of you and Tilly from that eagle cam went all over the world, in case you didn't know!"

"WHAT eagle cam!" Elmer demanded.

"You know there's a camera on the eagle's nest out there, and that you and Tilly were the stars of the show yesterday, right? Surely you did it on purpose! It would be impossible to get in the picture if you didn't know where the camera was!"

"Very funny," Elmer laughed. He was sure they were pulling his leg. "I can't wait to see this non-existent video!"

Al got out his phone and showed the footage he had saved from yesterday's eagle cam. Sure enough, there they were, chasing around the blanket and doing it in plain sight.

"Oh my god!" Elmer said. "Who else knows about this?"

"Well, it's all over the Internet, although I imagine only a few of your friends here in South Branch recognized who it was."

Elmer turned on his phone and opened the YouTube app. Sure enough, there was the video at the top of the "Trending Now" list. Not only that, but there were several copies to which random people had added fake voiceover narration and then reposted. Elmer tried the first one:

As the video played, Elmer listened to the fake sound track that someone had added- *"Welcome wildlife lovers! Naturalist O. Lordy here. In today's video, we see a pair of Homo sapiens engaging in their customary mating ritual and then copulating until the male has finally finished fucking his favorite female. The mating dance begins with the pair drinking fruit juice, which seems to serve as an aphrodisiac of some kind. The male, I'll call him Homo erectus, then begins to pursue the female around the colorful location that will be their nesting site. She runs away, but shows her interest in mating by turning and pursuing the male whenever he pauses in his pursuit. Watch this next part carefully! Here, we see them, partially aroused, take prone positions in the nest and begin rubbing their body parts together in a gesture that we naturalists call 'Making Out'. At the conclusion of this part of the ritual, the female awkwardly rolls onto her back, and applies some kind of liquid to her genitals. We have not yet discovered the purpose of this potion, but we think it may be a signal of readiness to the male since he mounts her a moment later.*

At first, it may appear from the movements of her extremities, that he is attacking her and that she is trying to get away! However, if we look closer, we can observe that once coitus begins, she envelops him with her upper and lower extremities so as to prevent him from leaving the scene before she is satisfied. The pair now engages in slow rhythmic movements, which continue for some time. We find that in younger members of the species, these movements are concluded much more quickly, however this mating pair is quite old and lack the vigor of younger subjects. I've edited the video here to eliminate the more repetitive and boring parts. Finally, the male begins more rapid movements, resulting in ejaculation. He then rolls off to rest as the female continues stimulating her genitals with a tool of some kind until she is fully satisfied as well. It's interesting to note that, even though the female is too old to bear offspring, the pair pursues this activity as enthusiastically as younger members of this species."

Elmer was shocked, but this was mitigated a bit by the cleverness of the fake narration. He breathed a sigh of relief that only a few people who happened to recognize them knew their identities.

That afternoon, Elmer reported on all this to Tilly, who, to his surprise, thought it was hilarious.

"Don't worry Elmer, it will all blow over by morning and we'll have a good laugh over it with the few people who know. I think it's fun to be anonymously world famous!"

Tilly wasn't so confident when they turned on the local evening news and saw a report of their exploits as the lead story. They also learned, to their dismay, that after their video went viral on the Internet, twelve additional couples were recorded doing the same thing by the eagle cam and it was reported that couples were waiting line for their turn at international fame.

The following day, a reporter for the South Branch Sentinel approached them for the inside story; apparently their names had gotten out. They declined the interview, but the next day, three days after their adventure, their pictures, which the paper had on file, appeared on the front page of the Sentinel under the headline, "Local couple, Tilly and Elmer Talbot, remain too modest to grant an interview after making South Branch, Iowa an international hot spot for viewing wildlife!"

After a few days, the story started to fade and Tilly and Elmer began to relax a little. Then, an official looking letter arrived. It was on the letterhead of NARC. This looked ominous until they discovered NARC was the North American Raptor Center.

"Dear Mr. and Mrs. Talbot:

It has come to our attention that you were the pair that was seen having sexual relations on one of our cameras near South Branch, Iowa last week. Your actions were unbelievable and unprecedented! Streaming video from this camera is available to anyone in the world who has access to the Internet and, as a result, thousands of viewers watched some or all of your 'performance'. In addition, reposted video clips of your activity reached many millions more! This is something we failed to foresee when we positioned cameras to capture never before seen video of animals in the wild. We have been in contact with professionals who have advised us as to the proper response to this event."

"Oh, oh! Here comes the lawsuit!" said Elmer as he read the letter to Tilly.

"The North American Raptor Center cannot thank you enough for your actions! As a result of your dramatic and brave performance, contributions to NARC over the past week have surpassed the entire total of contributions to our important work over the twenty-three years we have been in existence!

As a 'Thank You', NARC would like to invite you to spend a weekend at our 'Charles Thomson Center for Eagle Studies" in Washington D.C., at our expense. We'll also be making you lifetime members of NARC, and we will be requesting that our board of directors consider naming our South Branch camera and web location 'The Tilly and Elmer Talbot Wildlife Cam.'

Your efforts have been so important to our work here at

NARC, that have been advised by our financial consultants to offer you a generous contract to reprise your performance from time to time at our other eagle cam locations. These performances would be unannounced beforehand so as to increase viewership and, of course, to increase donations from appreciative wildlife enthusiasts around the world. Our council will be contacting you in a few days to begin a conversation about your availability, and your remunerative requirements, for the undertaking of this important project. Thank you again for your invaluable contributions to our studies of wildlife!"

"What's next?" they asked each other, just before the producers of "Good Morning America" called.

~~~

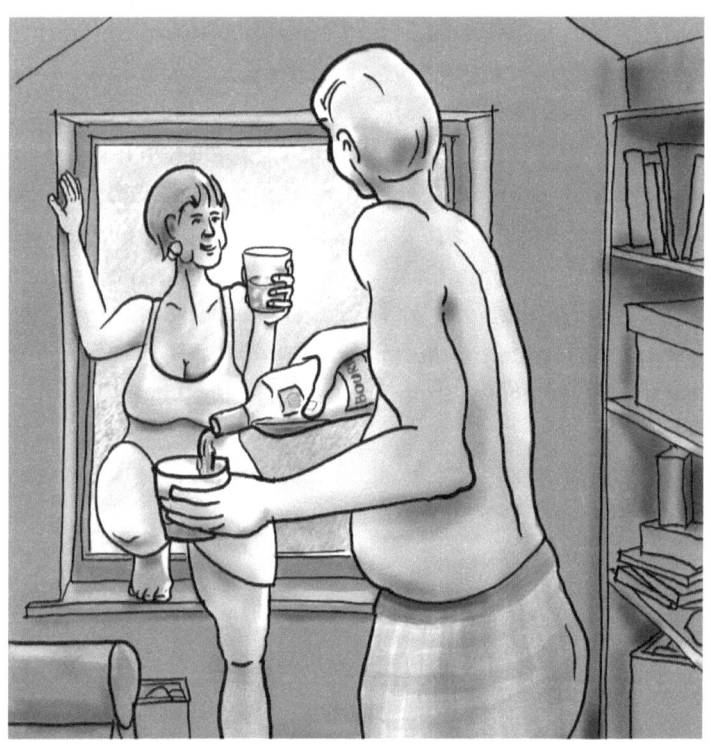

5
JUNE MONSOON

Elmer was enjoying the last few minutes of stolen sleep as he reluctantly let go of a sexy dream that he probably wouldn't be telling Tilly about. Once he realized that he was vaguely awake, and that Tilly was sitting up in bed next to him reading her romance novel, he felt a fleeting moment of concern that she might have been reading his mind while he enjoyed his naughty nocturnal canoodling with a girl he hadn't seen in half a century. Of course, Tilly was mentally canoodling with the shirtless and muscular hero depicted on the cover of the bodice ripper she was reading so he figured they were even.

A nearby flash of lightening and a nearly simultaneous crash of thunder interrupted their lightly lascivious illusory liaisons. This turned their attention to the sound of rain drumming against the bedroom window.

"Are you awake, Elmer?" Tilly asked.

"A little."

"That should be good enough. We have to finalize our plans for 'National Bourbon Day'!"

"We what?"

"It's June 14th, 'National Bourbon Day,' Elmer, and we have to decide how to celebrate!"

"I'd think it would be obvious how to celebrate 'National Bourbon Day'!" Elmer mused. "Don't we usually just spend the day drinking Bourbon?"

"Well, Elmer, in case you've forgotten, we usually 'celebrate' first and then drink Bourbon afterwards. When we've tried it the other way, we just fall asleep and never get around to 'celebrating'!"

"There's nothing wrong with sleeping?" Elmer asserted. He smiled to himself and gave Tilly's leg a squeeze. "But in our younger days, we never associated being in bed in the daytime with sleeping did we?"

"No we didn't Elmer! These aren't our younger days though, so we might have to sneak up on our 'National Bourbon Day' celebration."

"I propose we begin with breakfast!" he said. "Can we have Bourbon?"

"I'll put a little in the pancakes," Tilly said. "But if we have too much first, we'll forget to 'celebrate'!"

The pair had a leisurely meal in their bedclothes and recounted their customary method of celebrating. It was agreed that the "celebration" would begin a little later in the day, and after breakfast Tilly went back to her reading and Elmer ventured up to the attic to be sure the bucket they kept under the small leak in the roof was not overflowing. He was gone for some time, and eventually Tilly climbed the narrow stairway to see what he had gotten into.

Tilly had grown up in the century old house, whose basic structure was comprised of a simple, one story rectangle. A gable roof extended from the back of the house to the front, creating a dimly lit, tunnel like, attic. In contrast to the general darkness of the space, a

June Monsoon

window in the front, facing the county road a hundred yards away, and a matching window in the rear gable, facing south toward the backyard and the garage, fields, and woods beyond, created a usually sunny nook at each end. The sloping ceiling was sheathed with thin plywood, interrupted every three feet or so by beams just above Elmer's head height. The floor of the attic was made of wood planks, covered in some areas by throw rugs that were part of the chaotic collection of furnishings, household objects, and memorabilia stored there. Whenever either of them entered the attic, they felt a childlike delight with the secretive mystery evoked by the garret; not surprisingly, this was mixed with a momentary feeling that they should really get up there and clear out half the contents.

An old overstuffed loveseat resided next to the south window, in an alcove carved out of the hodgepodge of boxes and family heirlooms, and this provided a mostly private getaway for Tilly or Elmer to retire to when they needed some time to themselves or to engage in some kind of behavior that they realized their spouse would comment on if they knew about it. Tilly kept a supply of dark chocolate out of sight nearby while Elmer's small, ancient, but precious collection of Playboy magazines, contraband that he had kept hidden from his mother during his adolescence, now resided on the floor under the loveseat, although Tilly knew they were there. The nearby location of the bottle of expensive Bourbon, for use in case of emergency, was known to both of them.

"Are you perusing pictures of prehistoric playmates

47

featuring awesome airbrushed anatomy?" Tilly inquired.

"No, I'm looking at some even more titillating treasures! A couple of old love notes we wrote to each other back when we did that sort of thing."

"Where did you find those?" Tilly asked.

"In a box among the junk. I knew we had them somewhere but it's been decades since I came across them."

"We really should clean this place up, Elmer!"

"I'll do it tomorrow," he said with a laugh. "Look at these! They're notes we passed to each other back in high school! This one must have been one you wrote to me after we had gone out together a couple of times. Too bad neither of us put a date on any of them." Elmer handed her the note.

"Well, I guess we didn't think they would be historical artifacts some day!" Tilly laughed. She began to read aloud:

"Hi Elmer,

Halloween is almost here! Are you going to the Halloween Dance? I think it will be fun - if I have a date that is. What are you going as? I have an idea, but I'm not going to tell you what it is! You probably won't recognize me though!

See you in biology class this afternoon!

Your friend,

Tilly"

"I was a shameless flirt, wasn't I?" Tilly said.

"Not shameless enough for me to get it," Elmer laughed.

"You WERE a little dense, but I figured you'd eventually catch on. And I guess you did – you're sitting here with me fifty years later!" She gave his thigh a squeeze.

"That note probably scared me to death," Elmer said. "The Halloween dance was our third date, and I knew what was supposed to happen!"

"I did too Elmer, and my panties were wet when you finally did it!"

"My shorts were wet too, but that was because I almost peed my pants when you pushed me off the porch!"

"You know very well I didn't push you off the porch! But you would have deserved it, making me wait for that kiss out there in the cold while you were getting your nerve up."

"My nerve was the only thing I was having trouble getting up as I recall! And you know I fell totally in love with you that night don't you?"

Tilly laughed. "And by the time I got into the house, I was imagining us married with three children!" She leaned over and gave Elmer a kiss.

"Here's one I must have given you the next time I saw you in school after that night," Elmer said. "Notice that I was afraid to mention the actual kiss, lest you had hated it. Or maybe in case the note fell into the wrong hands!"

"Hi Tilly,

Saturday night was a lot of fun wasn't it? At least I thought so. I hope you thought it was fun too. I'll try not to scare you next time! If there IS a next time, which I hope there is.

Elmer"

"I was so thrilled and confused back then, Elmer. And so happy to anticipate having a real boyfriend who seemed to like me for myself and wasn't just interested in getting into my pants."

"I WAS just interested in getting into your pants, Tilly. But after you kissed me, I suddenly felt a responsibility to protect you from boys who just wanted to get into your pants. It was a strange time!"

"For both of us, Elmer!"

"I didn't find any more notes like that. I guess we just communicated using hand gestures from then on!"

Tilly gently placed her hand on his upper thigh and slid it slowly across his manhood. "Like this you mean?" she asked.

An involuntary expansion of his manly protuberance stood in for a verbal answer.

Tilly began to unbutton his pajama top. "We've had lots of fun on this old loveseat, haven't we Elmer?"

"That we have, but it's been a while."

"I think we should rectify that this afternoon, Elmer. Remember the first time we made love on this sofa?"

"I sure do," Elmer said, "that was scary!"

Tilly smiled and began kissing his now exposed belly. "After we went all the way for the first time, we never wanted to do anything else as I recall."

"Right, and, since it was winter, we were sometimes reckless about the venue. But I'll never forget the first time on this sofa. It was so cold outside we couldn't do it in the truck, so we sneaked back to your house late and did it on this couch when it used to be in the living room. That would have been a great idea – if your parents hadn't been 'sleeping' in the next room!"

"At least we thought they were 'sleeping'!" said Tilly. "Until my mom started telling my dad to fuck her harder and he began telling her just what he was going to do to her! I couldn't believe MY PARENTS were doing it!"

"And I was so startled by their voices at just the wrong time that I pulled out of you suddenly, which caused me to make a huge wet spot on the sofa! That complicated the issue since we had to try to clean it up without letting them know we were there or that we heard what they were doing. Very awkward all around."

Tilly and Elmer got up and examined the old sofa for any remaining evidence of this untidiness, finding traces of many spilled liquids, but none that they could connect to that particular affair.

Tilly stepped to the window and looked out. The lightening and thunder had moved east but the warm rain continued to come down steadily, drumming sensuously against the roof and making the little alcove and loveseat seem like a protected, secret hideaway, invulnerable to any disturbance from the outside world.

As she looked out, Elmer perched on the arm of the sofa and looked at her, silhouetted against the gray background outside, mentally comparing her shape and posture against the girl he had coupled with on this couch nearly fifty years before. Like the two of them, the sofa itself had been new and perky fifty years ago, and like the two of them, the sofa had begun to sag a bit and its surface was now dappled with blemishes, but despite the rough and tumble of daily life it was still comfortable and had adapted itself to the vagaries of those it came in contact with.

Tilly was dressed in an undecorated light pink nightgown that was silky and sexy. The garment extended only to her mid thigh and was loosely draped around her except where the soft undulating folds were pulled taught to reveal an attractive stretch across her breasts and hips. Elmer noted with pleasure that she was as beautiful now as she had been fifty years ago, an observation that he made often and that surprised him slightly every time. He stepped up behind her, reached around her waist, and pulled her body against his.

"It feels like you're ready for some excitement!" she giggled.

"I have a feeling we're both ready to have a nostalgic interaction with this old sofa, Tilly!"

They studied the furniture. "I remember when we used to come up here and make love on this old loveseat back when my folks had just moved south and we moved in, before we had kids."

"We gave it a workout in those days!"

"We were very inventive weren't we Elmer? I remember draping my front over the back facing away from you and spreading my legs so I could prop a foot against each arm while you came up behind me. I don't think I could hold myself in that position now though."

"And then there was the tricky thing we invented where you'd lie down with the back of your head on the seat, your back propped vertically against the seat back, and your legs flying up in space and wiggling around like rabbit ears in a windstorm while I approached you from different angles. We were pretty good at geometry back then, Tilly!"

"Definitely!" she agreed. "I'm ready to see if we can reprise that position right now!"

They tried to reenact this pose, but even with Elmer's help, Tilly couldn't get her backside high enough up the back of the sofa to make it work. They tried one or two more of their old favorite approaches to arranging their bodies over the loveseat for comfortable coupling, but each position was either painful or required so much stamina to hold themselves in the required contortion that they couldn't last long enough to enjoy a delightful dalliance.

"We might have to give up the idea of doing something unusual and just get into bed, Tilly," Elmer suggested.

"I know something we could do that wouldn't require superhuman strength, but it would be pretty nostalgic! Nostalgic, yet nearly unprecedented!" Tilly teased.

"Well?"

"Let's drag this throw rug out into the back yard for something to lay on and do it in the rain! We'll wear our nightclothes and everything will be soaked by the time we finish!"

"Hmmm!" Elmer said. "Have we ever done it in the rain before?"

"Only once that I can remember!"

Elmer thought a minute. "It could be kind of awful," he said.

"That would be a first – it's NEVER awful, Elmer. But if it doesn't work we'll just come inside, dry off, and figure out how to damage this sofa some more!"

Elmer wasn't fully convinced, but Tilly was known for having good ideas when it came to sexual shenanigans. "Ok, I guess I'm willing!" he said.

They rolled up the throw rug, carried it down the narrow stairway, and paused on the back porch, not sure whether this idea was sensational or senseless.

"Come on, Elmer, I can't wait all day for you to fuck me!" Tilly said.

Elmer knew that when she used that word he shouldn't hesitate. The warm rain was coming down steadily but gently and once they got used to it, the shower felt tingly and sexy. They spread out the rug over the wet grass and lay down, feeling the water soak through their thin clothing. Elmer rolled on top of Tilly, in part to protect her from the rain hitting her in the face. She was wearing a cute smile and Elmer studied how sexy she looked with her wet hair attractively splashed across the rug underneath.

Elmer pulled Tilly's short nightgown up above her breasts, then pushed his thin flannel PJs down to his mid thigh. He licked his fingers, quickly applied them to her pussy for a hint of lubrication beyond rainwater, and then slowly entered her so as to minimize any irritation. Rain softly pummeled his posterior, trickled and tickled its way down the crack of his ass, and around his testicles. Tilly wrapped her legs around his, interlocked her feet, placed her hands on the sides of his bottom, and began slowly guiding his movements to suit her desires.

"We did this fifty years ago, Wiggle Bare!" she said. "I'll entertain you with the story while you fuck me."

Tilly never used this kind of language except when she was especially aroused. He loved it when she did that, and she knew he loved it. Elmer raised his upper body and looked into her eyes as his manhood slowly teased her from the inside. "Oh, yes, Elmer, do it just like that!"

Tilly paused. "It was when you came to San Francisco to bring me back to South Branch after college. That was a long trip, and we hated each other at the beginning, before your truck broke down in the middle of Wyoming or wherever it was."

"Well, I was upset that you had taken up with all those dozens of San Francisco guys!" Elmer said. He forgot what he was doing and was still for a moment.

"Don't stop, Elmer," Tilly reminded him. "It wasn't dozens, but we can haggle over the exact number later!"

She recommended her manipulation of his backside.

"I didn't think much of you when we left San Francisco either, Elmer, but …," Tilly inhaled sharply and squeezed Elmer's ass involuntarily. "…but after the little incident with your truck, when we fell totally back in love with each other, the trip was more fun."

Elmer's respiration rate and the pace of his penetration quickened.

"And after that, we began trying to make up for four years of being apart!"

"I couldn't get enough of you, Tilly!"

"And you probably remember that I was encouraging you all the way!"

The pair individually fondled their own memories of that portion of the trip in their imaginations while they expertly moved together and apart as though they had practiced this dance five thousand times; which they had.

"Now do you remember that time in the rain?" Tilly asked, nearly out of breath.

"Oh my god, Tilly!" Elmer whispered. "We were on some back road, I had no idea where exactly since I was trying to get back to South Branch as slowly as possible. Somewhere in Nebraska I suppose, and it was raining and there was a wheat field next to the road…"

"And we never discussed it at all Elmer! You just pulled over and we both jumped out of the truck and ran into the field like we couldn't get into each other's pants fast enough. As soon as we were slightly out of sight in the tall wheat, we just pulled down as little clothing as we had to and you started fucking me like it was our last five minutes on earth!"

Elmer was breathing as though he had just run across that wheat field.

"I remember how beautiful you looked, (deep breath) soaking wet like that. Like now!"

"I loved that Elmer! Your cock was playing with the inside of my cunt and the rain was soaking my clothes and running down all over us. I was so hot I could have screamed!"

"You did scream, sweetheart! And the pleasure of making you feel that way pushed me over the edge. I filled you up with probably the most copious contribution I've ever made to the cause."

Elmer was about to try matching that moment.

By now, Tilly was breathing too rapidly to speak clearly, but she did manage to make some sounds that Elmer correctly interpreted as, "Keep that up for about two more seconds and I'll be screaming again." Elmer watched the random, involuntary expressions cross Tilly's face like the drifting clouds overhead; a look of pleading, then mild pain, then astonishment, then sadness, then wide eyed delight. Tilly shut her eyes tight and positioned her arm across her face. She began gasping for breath, making little sounds, and squirming uncontrollably. This activity concluded with a look of pure joy on her face. As it had fifty years before, watching Tilly's pleasure caused Elmer to lose control of his body as well. Without conscious thought, it went through a familiar program of hard breathing, rhythmic contractions of particular muscles, giving way to the unexpected production of unintelligible sounds, followed by shivering and then by random, uncontrollable convulsions surging across his abdomen. This program culminated in his seeming to lose all strength and collapsing on top of Tilly like a rag doll. Tilly held him tight and Elmer began giggling uncontrollably.

"That's exactly what you did back then, Elmer," Tilly said. "It seemed like you were so happy you couldn't keep it inside and that's just the way it got expressed."

"Apparently it still works that way!" Elmer whispered.

"I like hearing you giggling after we do it Elmer. It lets me know how much you liked it!" said Tilly.

Tilly and Elmer held each for some time, feeling the rain massaging their tired bodies and enjoying the tickling trickle of rivulets working their way across their skin.

"I like hearing you giggle too, Tilly. And I know just how to make that happen at this point in the proceedings!"

"How?"

"By going inside and pouring two glasses of Bourbon!"

~~~

6

FOURTH OF JULY FIREWORKS

Elmer was flattered at first. As a result of a chance meeting in Pearl's Downtown Diner with the mayor of South Branch, Elmer found himself appointed chairman of the Fourth of July Parade Committee! Elmer knew the Mayor casually, but he had never been appointed to any civic position and so he was looking forward to the opportunity, albeit somewhat warily. He had agreed to the proposition after a short conversation with the mayor, who told him most of the work was handled every year by his staff and that the main thing Elmer had to do was wave to the crowd from an open convertible and appoint the young lady who would have the honor of portraying Betsy Ross on the float that was the centerpiece of the parade. It was traditional to choose the prettiest girl from the high school graduating class for this sought-after honor; auditioning a half dozen or so cute and vivacious eighteen-year-old young women seemed like an agreeable way to perform one's civic duty. Elmer was right to be a bit wary – he was soon to discover that "sought-after" could be more accurately described as "fought-over".

Elmer couldn't wait to announce his new civic responsibility to Tilly, who found it mildly amusing. Unlike Elmer, she had some knowledge of the competition to be cast as Betsy Ross, and she knew that some of the young ladies, and their mothers, attempted to secure the honor in ways that were far from ladylike. For his part, Elmer enjoyed regaling his friends with the details of his new assignment, at least before the actual auditions began.

The day after his informal meeting with the mayor, Elmer had an appointment with the Mayor's assistant, Hilda, a rather stern but efficient woman who explained the process. She and her staff took care of most elements of the parade. These were cut and dried and were repeated year after year; the call to the high school band leader, the heads of the various civic clubs in town, and the invitation to local car dealers who supplied automobiles for use in the parade as a means of advertising. Even the Betsy Ross float was taken care of by a local farmer who had originally built a float out of a farm wagon which he pulled with his tractor, but who had now reconfigured the remains of an automobile he had saved from the junkyard, after its roof had been flattened in an unfortunate incident, and built a proper platform for Betsy on the top. This he upgraded during the winter months and he took pride in driving the contraption in the parade every summer.

Elmer was provided with a temporary office in the basement of City Hall, use of an office computer, a city email address, and a mailbox in the main office. He was somewhat surprised that the primary directive during his orientation to the job was not to be intimidated by the mothers of the candidates and to choose the lady who would best represent the city of South Branch and attract the largest possible attendance. It had become apparent over the years that the skimpier Betsy's costume became the more excitement surrounded the parade, although there was a tipping point beyond which the costume could become a minor scandal, so this was a narrow target. As part of the audition, the young ladies were to design their proposed costume and, in theory, they were to construct the garment themselves. This all seemed like fun to Elmer and he formally accepted the position which was to be noted in the South Branch Sentinel the next day.

When Elmer got home that afternoon, ready to

describe his new duties, Tilly told him that she had already taken a message from one of the candidate's mothers who had requested that Elmer give her a call.

"My appointment hasn't even been reported in the paper yet!" he said.

"Get used to it Elmer!" she laughed.

When Elmer called the lady back, Tilly listened to his half of the conversation:

"Hello. Is this Mrs. NO•nickers?"

"Oh, Mrs. NONIK•ers! I'm sorry! This is Elmer Talbot. I understand you left a message for me to call."

"Thank you! Yes, it is an honor to be appointed to head the Fourth of July Parade committee."

"She was? That's very impressive for a girl of eighteen! I'll definitely be interested in looking at Destiny's application!"

"That must have been difficult as a single mom!"

"Yes, I'm sure you do need a man around now and then when things come up that you'd rather not have to take care of yourself!"

"Good. I'm looking forward to meeting you and Destiny!"

"Right. Good Bye."

"How did this woman get my name do you think, Tilly?" Elmer asked. "She was sure lobbying for her daughter to play Betsy Ross!"

"Well, Elmer, I hear some moms take this competition to be a big deal! The way I hear it, they've been known to try bribing the parade chairman!"

"I'll look forward to that," Elmer said. "Chastity suggested she might like to entertain me in private one of these days!"

"Chastity?"

"Chastity No-nickers. Rather an oxymoronic moniker it seems," Elmer noted, although Tilly didn't seem to find this especially funny.

The next afternoon, Elmer's new position was mentioned in the "South Branch Sentinel". This resulted in an outpouring of congratulations from his buddies and an outpouring of attention from ambitious mothers of recent female high school graduates. Within a few minutes of the Sentinel's publication, Elmer began receiving texts from middle aged women (who were the age of his daughter) regarding the virtues of their female offspring, and not so delicately suggesting some favors they might be willing grant him in exchange for a favorable appraisal of their daughters' assets.

Helo Mr. Talbot. This is Summer Melones I m glad u r chairman of the parade. I m sure we r going 2 b VERY good friends! I wnt 2 meet u and sho u Missy Melones! She shoud b Betsy Ross! I will sho u my Melones 2 ha ha!

Elmer was delighted and when he got home, he read this text to Tilly, thinking she would find it amusing. She didn't. The next day, Elmer found an envelope in his office mailbox and put it in his briefcase, then absent mindedly left it with the stack of unopened mail on the kitchen table when he got home. As it happened, Tilly opened the letter and, upon seeing the contents, read it aloud to Elmer:

"Good afternoon, Mr. Talbot,

Congratulations on your appointment to the post of Fourth of July Parade Chairman by my friend, Mayor Meyer! I'm writing to introduce my daughter, Candice Quimby, a recent graduate of South Branch High. Of course we think she is talented and beautiful, but we are not alone; she has won many awards for her scholarship, beauty, and civic engagement, including being named to the Dean's list each year, being elected Homecoming Queen last fall, and serving as president of the South Branch Beautification Club at SBH. In addition, she is a gifted fashion designer and seamstress! Naturally, we believe these qualities will make her a leading candidate for the role of Betsy Ross in the Fourth of July Parade!"

"This girl sounds pretty good!" Tilly said.

She continued reading:

"On a related note, I believe you were a classmate of Susan Bell, Candice's grandmother! Susan usually spends her summers at our secluded beach house in Wisconsin and I'm sure she would be delighted to 'entertain' you there if you were able to get away for a week or two this summer! I'm sure the two of you have a lot to catch up on!

All good wishes,

Scarlett Quimby, Esq."

"That sounds like fun," Elmer said as a joke. In fact he was taken aback. Not only was Susan Bell his former classmate, he had had a hopeless crush on her that had been the major focus of his erotic high school fantasies until he connected with Tilly! Tilly knew about his high school crush on "Suziebelle" and she and Elmer had joked about it until Susan had shown up at their fiftieth high school reunion and seemed ready to remove the "hopeless" assumption. They had seemed to enjoy each other's company a little too much and their parting hug had looked a little too intimate, and lasted a little too long, for Tilly's taste.

"Oh, I'm sure it would be loads of fun!" Tilly said sarcastically before pointedly leaving the room.

They spent an uncommunicative evening together and Tilly noticeably ignored him except for a steely glare whenever his phone signaled an incoming text or e-mail. Elmer was feeling a bit overwhelmed by the constant flow of improper offers from middle-aged mothers, but this was mitigated somewhat by the flattering nature of their steamy suggestions and he couldn't help allowing himself a smile now and then as he pictured participating in some of the preposterous propositions. His occasional smiling responses to what Tilly correctly guessed were indecent ideas didn't improve their momentary enmity.

After a couple of weeks, Elmer had received several unexpected gifts of alcohol, suggestive e-mailed photos, promised meals at out of the way restaurants, and coupons for unspecified "personal services". He had also received six applications from young women for the position of "Betsy Ross" in the parade. In addition to the "curriculum vita" of each applicant, the submissions included designs for their proposed costumes. The popular method of submitting these designs was to have someone, (hopefully MOM) take a photograph of the young lady in her underwear, and then to draw the costume over this photo using some kind of digital painting software. These were sent via e-mail and Elmer discovered that in some cases, the costume overlay could be hidden to reveal the underlying photo. Elmer reluctantly "flattened" these photos on his computer so as to minimize any misadventures.

He found it necessary to reject three of the young applicants since their proposed costumes, while imaginative and delightful, were too risqué to meet what Elmer knew would comprise South Branches' "community standards". He briefly considered the advantages of moving to a different community where the "community standards" would embrace costumes consisting of a red baseball cap, a white bra, and scanty blue panties; an American Flag in which the white stars and white stripes were removed in favor of transparent fishnet material, allowing shifting views of the wearer's bare skin and white underthings, or a collection of small flags, fastened to several leather straps encircling the young lady's body and which, as they fluttered in the breeze, created a phantasmagoric yet patriotic peep show.

The remaining three candidates, Destiny Nonickers, Missy Melones, and Candice Quimby, were invited, along with their mothers, to meet Elmer for a final presentation of their qualifications. Elmer considered various options as to where this event might take place. There was no proper place in City Hall, and he didn't want the male staff to crash the party and offer improper influence, not to mention comments, during what was a serious occasion. He also worried that the young women might be intimated by the formality of City Hall. His solution was to hold the presentation in his backyard so as to make it as informal as possible. This venue would also have the advantage that Tilly would be present, and he didn't want her to fear he might be caving in to any improper influence.

The girls were instructed to wear at least a rough version of their proposed costume, which dictated, at a minimum, a modest degree of dignity, but their mothers were under no such restrictions and appeared in the raciest regalia they were willing to risk wearing in public. In addition, each mother brought a gift for Elmer, and each gift consisted of a bottle of expensive alcohol. Elmer hadn't anticipated that the presentation would devolve into a demonstration of debauchery, but once the mothers began a side competition as to who could concoct the tastiest toxic tipple, the downhill decent of the proceedings had begun. Tilly observed the events but remained aloof from participating. Elmer thought it would be unfair to show any favoritism when sampling the alcoholic offerings, and the mothers followed his lead in this momentary camaraderie. This portion of the party, however, was the last to feature this veneer of friendliness.

The girls, of course, were under age and Tilly, seeing the need to try to maintain some semblance of propriety in her own backyard, served the girls lemonade, but as the adults grew more distracted, the girls had no hesitation about topping up their glasses from some of the assorted bottles on the picnic table.

Elmer's plan was to seat everyone in a circle of lawn chairs and have a decorous discussion of the proposals as each girl modeled her costume. This took some time to organize as the drinking contest seemed more interesting, and each mother and daughter demanded Elmer's intimate attention so they could hug or kiss him, rub his bottom or hair, and take selfies with him in various compromising positions. Intermixed with these unladylike activities were whispered improper propositions. Elmer's head was spinning. He knew he had to bring some order to the proceedings and that he was going to be in enough trouble with Tilly as it was. Finally, Elmer asked the young ladies who were at least partly sober to arrange the lawn chairs in a circle so they could get the main event under way, and this slowly began to take place once Tilly left her perch on the back porch and began helping arrange things.

Finally, everyone was seated, and Tilly withdrew leaving the carryings on in Elmer's hands. Elmer couldn't help but notice that several of the participants had arranged their positions so that he could avail himself of an intimate view of her panties or verify without any doubt that she had left her bra at home. This in itself became a competition. Buttons were unbuttoned, legs were repositioned, skirts were hiked up. Tilly took note of the fact that Elmer didn't admonish them or make any attempt to look elsewhere. By now, Elmer was definitely destined for the doghouse.

The first girl arose to begin the presentation of her costume concept, and this went well for forty-six seconds before someone commented too loudly, "That looks like something a slut would wear!" The model tearfully returned to her seat as her tears turned toward treachery. The presentations became more raucous and comments that should have remained unexpressed were vocalized. The mostly calm discussion was now being carried on in loud voices and candidates and their mothers began to be labeled "Tramps", Sluts", or "Whores". Even the previously proper Scarlett Quimby could be heard calling her former friend Chastity Nonickers a "Fucking Bitch"! Elmer was about to declare the event over when Summer Melones rose to whisper a question to Elmer about the location of the bathroom. As she did so, Chastity stood up to chastise her and, in the process, tripped over Candice Quimby's outstretched and widely spread legs, causing her to trip and land in the lap of Missy Melones! This inaugurated the melee.

Elmer quickly retreated to the picnic table and rescued the open bottles from their perilous positions, then took refuge with Tilly on the porch for their personal safety. The pugilism persisted. It was fortunate that those mothers who had arrived in spiky high heels lost them early on in the fight lest some participants might have been accidently stabbed. Even so, the spectacle of a sextet of mothers and daughters entangled in hair pulling, clothes ripping mounds of madness was remarkably entertaining. Even Tilly, who was furious at Elmer for loving the licentious attention, later admitted the fight was quite a spectacle.

Finally, the fisticuffs ended when everyone was exhausted, and Tilly and Elmer sallied forth to assess the damage.

It appeared that there were no serious bodily injuries, however there was considerable property damage, primarily to the participants' clothing. The three young women, whose costumes had been loosely sewn together in anticipation of needing modification, found their creations in tatters on the ground, revealing the underwear of those girls that were wearing any. The three mothers, who were more sturdily clothed, were a bit more decent, although two blouses and a skirt were scattered across the lawn and curiously, a single nylon stocking was found hanging from a nearby tree limb. Any clothing that managed to remain in place was in need of laundering.

As the competitors got to their feet and collected their wits and clothing, Tilly went into the house and returned with an armload of towels for use as temporary coverings and then put her nursing skills to use in applying antiseptic and band-aids where needed. Meanwhile, Elmer called the mayor and arranged for him to dispatch a city van to pick up the remains of the candidates and deliver them to their places of residence since none was in any condition to drive.

When the combatants had been removed from the arena, Elmer turned to Tilly, expecting additional hostilities.

"I'm sorry Tilly. You know I would never take any of those people up on their propositions, don't you?"

"Not even a week at a secluded cabin with Suziebelle?"

"Tilly, I'd never even consider spending a week alone with Suziebell; I'd be worn out after our first couple of days together!"

"Oh! Well I guess a couple of days would be OK. And I could go over to Omaha for a visit with Buff Stevens and give him an opportunity to try out those shenanigans I wouldn't let him get by with fifty years ago."

"I don't think that would be a good idea Tilly! He might expire from the excitement!" Elmer chuckled.

As the sun began to set, Tilly and Elmer went outside, gathered up the fragments of red, white, and blue costumes, and brought them into the house where Tilly removed her dress and playfully began holding up various swatches of fabric in front of her, laughing as she used tape to hold them in place as she pieced together a patchwork garment. Elmer regarded her work.

"Tilly, it doesn't say anywhere that Betsy Ross has to be a young woman. As far as that goes, I've always pictured Betsy Ross as a grandmother. I think YOU should be Betsy Ross!"

"That would be a SCANDAL!" Tilly pointed out. "A shocking concoction of nepotism and naughtiness!"

"Perfect!" said Elmer. "And anyway, it won't be as much of a scandal as what just happened. That gossip is probably making the rounds already! I think you should do it! And you could sew up that patchwork costume which is probably more in keeping with what actually happened in those days."

"Are you offering me the position?" Tilly asked.

"Yes, but you'll have to bribe me with a night of wild sex to seal the deal!"

"Ha. I knew the whole thing was rigged. But what if I wear you out before your trip to visit Suzibelle?"

"She can be Betsy Ross a year from now!" he said.

"OK, Elmer. I'll go for the night of wild sex. But Suziebelle might be disappointed next year."

"Why?"

"Because if you give me the role of Betsy this summer, there isn't a chance you'll be appointed parade chairman again next year!"

"Good. That will be yet another benefit to giving you the part!"

~~~~

7
A Fair Affair

"Do you have your list, Elmer?" Tilly said as they got ready to go.

"I don't need a list, Tilly! I like to just wander around the fair and follow whatever catches my eye!"

"What do you think will catch your eye first, Elmer? Some young woman in short shorts or a foot-long corn dog?"

Elmer laughed. "Come on Tilly, I'm not that bad!

From time to time, I like to go look at the restored antique tractors or admire the artwork exhibit."

"I remember! Especially when the line to the "Corn Dog Castle" and the conveniently nearby "Tower of Tater Tots" passes right by the art show!" Tilly noted.

"Don't forget the 'Pork Chop Palace'! But I liked the art too, especially the shapes of some of the painters!"

"You're hopeless, Elmer!"

"No, I'm not! I'm quite hopeful that the "Apple Pie a la mode Milk Shake" place is there again this year. Those are especially good with the optional half cup of added Bourbon! So, what's on your list this year, Tilly?"

"Well, I love the quilts! I think I might get into quilting one of these days! And for some reason I can't resist the building where people exhibit their collections. People collect the strangest things."

Elmer agreed. "I remember the beer bottle caps and the collection of match book covers where you had to ask the guy to open up the book of racy ones! That was kind of hilarious!"

"I always like the ordinary household objects," Tilly said. "Like the souvenir salt and pepper shakers or the old bottles that strange pills came in."

"Remember when we were teenagers and we went to the fair together those two summers, Elmer? That was so much fun. And we couldn't stand to be out of sight of each other for one minute could we? You were the only exhibit I was interested in!"

"Right, and I felt the same about you Tilly! Plus, I

loved showing you off, like I had teamed up with the cutest girl in the county!"

"We must have been so cute!" Tilly said.

"We're still cute, Tilly! And I still love showing you off."

"Good. Maybe I should go over and hang out with the antique tractors! All the old men would think I fit right in!"

As usual, the fair was hot, exciting, and crowded. Perfect! They agreed to head off to follow their own interests, then meet for a mid-afternoon meal at the Corn Dog Castle, although Tilly was smart enough not to ingest any of their offerings.

After they completed their solo sojourns, they spent the remainder of the day wandering together, holding hands, and imagining it was the summer of their high school romance. Tilly and Elmer had one thing in particular that they always did together at the fair, but Elmer suggested that their traditional ride on the Ferris Wheel should wait until he had finished digesting a significant portion of the "Corn Dog Confrontation" and the "Tater Tot Tornado". They could then complete any desired amusement park rides before he headed to the Apple Pie and Bourbon Milk Shake stand for dessert. While Elmer was digesting, they walked around the fair, took note of the surprising enterprises people had thought of to extract money from the assembled fairgoers, regarded the various displays, and smiled at the young couples doing just what they had done fifty years before.

They sat down to look at the schedule of upcoming events for the afternoon and evening.

"I see Reverend Goode is going to be delivering a sermon at the 'Salvation Station' later, Tilly noted. "What do you think Elmer – that or the demolition derby?"

"I view the violent smashing of vintage vehicles as being very spiritual," Elmer said.

"Speaking of spiritual enlightenment, isn't that Gilt and Innocence over at the beer tent?" Tilly asked.

"Who and what?"

"Innocence Goode, Reverend Goode's daughter. She just graduated from South Branch High and she's working at 'Claire's Hair Affair' this summer. I get the impression she's not quite as innocent as her name suggests. And – it looks like Gilt's her latest boyfriend. Don't they look cute together Elmer?"

"Gilt and Innocence? A match made in heaven! How did he get that name?"

"Gilbert Tompkins. It became 'Gil T.' in school and then his friends just shortened it to 'Gilt'. From what I hear, he's a very sweet boy and isn't likely to be guilty of anything too serious."

"Well, Tilly, judging from the large beers they're carrying, they are at least guilty of underage drinking!"

"Not that we didn't tip a few before it was fully legal, Elmer! I think they're so cute and so in love I can't help but smile!"

Eventually Elmer felt his stomach could be trusted on the Ferris wheel and they got into line for the ride. They especially liked this amusement for two reasons: First, it took the riders to the highest point around and this allowed a view of the entire fairgrounds as well as the surrounding area. Second, once riders were elevated above the eye level of those on the ground, couples could engage in a brief period of naughty necking on each rotation. The second time Tilly and Elmer had ridden a Ferris Wheel together, just before she left South Branch for nursing school in San Francisco fifty years ago, she had teased him by removing her panties once they were out of public view at the top and they still practiced this tradition.

The Ferris Wheel was set up next to a pedestrian walkway through the fairgrounds and just next to Reverend Goode's "Salvation Station". This venue consisted of a tent roughly the size of a two-car garage, with a storage area behind that was surrounded by a canvas fence, but open to the sky. The tent itself was closed by canvas walls that could be opened to reveal a pulpit at the back and hay bales arranged in front for seating during the Reverend's presentations. The open storage area behind held additional hay bales, cartons of literature for distribution, and containers of merchandise that the Reverend offered for sale during and after his performances, including towels featuring an embroidered picture of the Reverend in the corner. These he bought from a Chinese company for seventy-five cents and, after adding value by blessing each carton, sold to the faithful for $19.95 each. He also sold framed photos of himself with inspiring sayings, as well as coffee cups, T-shirts, and his autographed monographs on morality.

When their turn came, Tilly and Elmer climbed aboard, lurching forward once they were settled and then stopping at a height of ten feet while the next gondola was unloaded, and new passengers were escorted aboard. During this pause, they had a view of the "Salvation Station" from the back and, as they watched, a young couple slipped, otherwise unnoticed, under the canvas fence of the storage enclosure. By the time Tilly and Elmer paused at the next higher position on the path of their conveyance a half minute later, it was apparent that the trespassers were Gilt and Innocence, and that they were not there to seize anything, apart from each other. The Ferris Wheel moved again to load more passengers and from their new, higher, position they could see that the nearly unnecessary foreplay had commenced with kissing and urgent hugs. Rising again for the next pause, they reached the summit of the Ferris Wheel's orbit. Now their aerial view revealed that the young lover's hands were already touching each other in a way that suggested their immediate goal was to locate the fasteners holding one another's clothing in place.

"These kids don't waste any time, do they Tilly?" Elmer noted.

"I don't either, Elmer!" Tilly said, handing him her panties.

Tilly and Elmer began traveling with their backs to

the path of travel as the ride began a descent to ground level again with two more stops to pick up the remaining passengers for this run, whereupon it continued in a slow, smooth rotation. On each round, Tilly and Elmer had a minute or so of a shifting but clear view of the action and another minute of descending travel when their view only offered glimpses of the action in the holy enclosure through the movement of gondolas on their upward path in front of them. Far from being disdainful of the antics of the lovers, Tilly and Elmer were delighted by the memories of their younger days that the activities brought forth.

"I wonder if they don't know people can watch them from the Ferris Wheel, or if they know and don't care!" Tilly mused.

"Well, Tilly, that's probably the most secluded place they had access to, and they just couldn't wait any longer. We were pretty reckless now and then when we were eighteen as I recall!"

"I know, Elmer! I'll never forget our very first attempt to go all the way in your basement when your folks come home, and your dad came downstairs and caught us half dressed. He saved us from real trouble when he told us to put our clothes on and sneak out while he distracted your mother, who would have killed us!"

As Tilly and Elmer alternated periods of clear views of the tryst and periods when their view was obscured, the mischief makers removed or repositioned the majority of their clothing and reclined on top of a stack of hay bales. It seemed clear that Innocence was the least innocent of the two and she positioned herself on top of Gilt, who was obviously abundantly agreeable.

After a few rotations the Ferris Wheel began pausing again to unload the passengers from this cycle and Tilly and Elmer were intending to quickly buy another ticket so they could continuing watching the show, when they saw Reverend Goode's pickup truck drive up behind the "Salvation Station"! It appeared that the "Salvation Station" might soon become the "Damnation Station".

"This is going to get ugly!" Tilly said. "I know about this guy – he's the biggest philanderer in town but in public he's obsessed with chastising anybody who likes any kind of sex. If he sees his daughter getting it on behind his "Salvation Station" he might strangle both of them!"

"Do you have an idea how we could rescue them?" Elmer asked. "We could 'pay it forward' for our teenaged rescue by my dad!"

They quickly devised a plan whereby Elmer, who had never met the Reverend, would nevertheless try to intercept him and cause a distraction while Tilly went around to the back of the open enclosure in an attempt to alert the rebellious rapscallions.

This plan could have worked. However, as they stepped off the ride, they saw the Reverend get in the short line for tickets to the Ferris Wheel instead of heading directly to his tent. If he got on the ride, he would be in position to observe his daughter and her evil-doing lover having premarital sex, a mortal sin in his opinion. This transgression would be made exponentially worse by the fact that anyone on the Ferris Wheel could see them; the scandal involving his daughter would all over town by nightfall!

"Plan B Elmer!" Tilly said. "I'll distract the Reverend while you go tell them to get out of there!"

Even this plan was nearly dashed; by the time Tilly caught up with the Reverend in hopes of keeping him off the Ferris Wheel, he had already bought his ticket and was waiting to get on the conveyance.

"Are you riding by yourself Reverend?" she asked.

"Yes, I love Ferris Wheels. The view is so interesting!" he told her.

"You'll find the view fascinating this time!" Tilly thought.

"Would you mind waiting for a second so I can ride with you?" she asked. "I have a question I need to discuss with you right away regarding sexual morality!"

Reverend Goode couldn't resist this request, both because he wanted to explain the particulars of sexual morality to her and because he was hoping he would be able to look down her blouse as he did so.

"Of course, my child!" he said, even though he was thirty years younger than Tilly.

"Oh, thank you, Reverend!" she told him. "I'm in desperate need of your council. I'll just grab a ticket and be right back."

This gambit gave Tilly about a half a minute to acquire the required ticket, figure out what her morality question was, and devise a way to keep him from looking over to the enclosure behind the "Salvation Station" once their seat was airborne. When Tilly returned with her ticket and the pair stepped on to the ride, Tilly insisted on sitting on the left side since if the Reverend was looking toward her in that location, he would be somewhat less likely to see the young lovers below. Tilly had to work fast; once the contraption rotated though even one basket position the young couple's hideaway would be visible.

"Reverend Goode, I have to tell you that these rides scare me to death. I can't look down at the ground or I might become sick to my stomach! I always feel like I might fall out, even with this metal bar across our laps!"

She grabbed the metal bar, 'accidentally' grasping the upper portion of Reverend Goode's thigh along with it.

"Don't worry, my dear, you'll be safe with me!" the Reverend said, putting his arm around her shoulder affectionately. "Now, what's this sinful morality question that's on your mind?"

They were reaching the point where, if the Reverend looked ahead and to his right, he'd see his daughter's debauchery.

"Look at me Reverend!" Tilly said. "Promise me you'll never reveal the sin I'm about to disclose to anyone! I would be mortified if anyone in South Branch were to find out!"

"You can confess anything to me, child. I'm forbidden by God to reveal anything I hear in confidence!"

Since Tilly had heard rumors that she knew had started with Reverend Goode, she assumed that God wasn't particularly strict on this point, but in spite of this she knew she had to keep the Reverend's attention focused on her for several minutes. Tilly also knew it would be increasingly windy at their seat as the Ferris Wheel gained elevation, and that her panties were in Elmer's pocket far below. She considered for a moment the probability that what she was about to say would make her the most talked about sexagenarian in South Branch, but, if she wanted to rescue the cute young lovers below from a devastating fate, this was her best chance. And anyway, a good scandal might give her some status among a certain class of South Branch citizens!

"Oh, Reverend Goode, I have a terrible secret! But since you're a man of the cloth, I'm sure you've never heard of anything this sinful before!" She looked at him piteously and squeezed his thigh, moving her hand in slightly closer proximately to his manhood. A movement under his clothing suggested he was becoming quite interested in her story. "But I just don't think I can tell you my dreadful secret!"

Meanwhile, Elmer had moved just outside the canvas enclosure surrounding the spur-of-the-moment sanctuary. The fence was too high for him to look over, and he didn't want to shout at the youngsters lest others would hear. He needed to get their attention without alerting anyone else nearby. Elmer figured he'd be able to toss something over the fence and get their attention, but what? He searched the grounds nearby for some piece of litter that he could pelt the perpetrators with to get their attention. The area appeared unexpectedly tidy, until he spied two half-filled cups of beer near the fence where he and Tilly had seen the lovers scramble under!

Keeping his arm around her, the Reverend placed his free hand on her shoulder and began massaging it gently. "Don't worry, my child. Go ahead and tell me everything! It will make you feel so much better to get this off your lovely chest."

Tilly wondered about his continuing habit of referring to her as a child. And now he was admiring her tits!

"I know you want to help. And I did come to you with this problem, but I'm just too upset to tell you. I'm sorry! I can only say it has something to do with my sexual feelings!"

The Ferris Wheel had made the first of its complete revolutions for this cycle and by now, Tilly could tell that the Reverend was paying no attention to anything outside their gondola.

"Sexual feelings can be confusing and complicated!" he said. "But it's very important to seek council from an expert on sexual sin in order to get onto the proper path!"

"Can you show me what to do?" Tilly asked.

"Trust me, sweetheart. Your afterlife could depend on telling me what's bothering you!" the Reverend said ominously!

Elmer thought sloshing the remaining beer over the

fence could get the miscreant's attention, but he still couldn't see over the fence. In the absence of something to climb on, he thought of a periscope, but of course, he didn't happen to have a periscope with him. He thought of taking a photo of the couple with his phone and this gave him an idea; he could turn on the camera in his phone and lift the device above the fence, thereby seeing the camera's view on the screen. Could he use this view to aim the flinging of beer to alert the couple? He held the cup and, looking at the screen on his phone, attempted to launch the contents over the fence and onto the bare skin of the amatory adolescents. This, however, caused only a momentary pause in the proceedings since most of the beer landed on their clothing on the ground next to them.

"Everyone knows that you're an expert on sin, Reverend Goode! It's just that this is so embarrassing. It has to do with …, with something I shouldn't do except with my husband!"

"It's OK, Tilly. Many of my female parishioners are tempted to engage in sinful acts with men outside their marriage. Some are even attracted to me! Can you imagine that? It's nothing to be ashamed of! Sometimes I need to spend considerable time with them to explore all the evils of this undesirable desire. But they always come around."

Tilly tried to suppress a smile. *I shouldn't think it would take them long to see the flaw in THAT desire!*" she thought.

The Ferris Wheel passed the top of its path and

started down again.

"Thank you for being so kind to me Reverend!" She moved her hand higher on his thigh and squeezed as though she might fall out of the gondola if she became any more upset! The gondola reached the bottom level and started up again where even a glance in the wrong direction could alert the Reverend to the scenario of sin currently being carried out next door. She looked directly at the Reverend.

"All right, I'll tell you!" Tilly paused to take a deep breath. "I seem to have an unnatural desire to show off my private parts to strange men!" A tear came to her eye. "I can't help it Reverend. I want them to look at me and imagine doing immoral things to me. And…" She was on a roll now. "And what's worse, I like to imagine them actually DOING those things. It makes me feel SO sinful!" Tilly shivered in a way that the Reverend interpreted as an expression of remorse.

The Reverend was taken aback. She needed his "counseling" all right, he thought! He turned his head as though about to look out over the landscape to give her a minute to rest before he began to advise her.

"OH!" Tilly squealed.

The Reverend quickly turned back to see what was wrong before he had time to notice his offspring getting off in the enclosure next door. The hem of Tilly's skirt was raised up over the safety bar across their laps, revealing her upper thighs. Even worse, since her panties were safely resting in Elmer's pocket, this unexpected situation also caused the sparse gray "maidenhair" covering her pubic mound to be prominently displayed to the minister!

"It was the wind, Reverend Goode!" she said apologetically, making no move to relocate the wayward garment.

"I'm sure it was," said the Reverend sympathetically. "You don't need to worry; I've seen many women without their underwear!" He wondered if this had come out as a reassuring revelation, as he had intended.

Tilly put her hands over her face as though to hide her embarrassment, giving the Reverend plenty of time to study the forbidden regions of her anatomy. Their compartment was now nearing the platform where they were to disembark, so to avoid any embarrassment to himself, he delicately grasped the hem of Tilly's dress and lowered it gently to its properly modest position.

"We need to get off now, child!" he said quietly.

"Oh, yes!" she said in a way that could be easily misconstrued.

Elmer retrieved the last partially filled cup from the ground and made a final bid to douse the debauchers. This time, Innocence's back and Gilt's legs were sufficiently splattered to get their attention and they turned to see Elmer's hand above the fence, alternately making the sign of the cross and then pointing in the direction of the Ferris Wheel. The lovers leaped up and approached the fence where they could now hear Elmer quietly admonishing them to skedaddle or face the wrath of Reverend Goode. In spite of the need for haste, the chaotic collecting of their clothing and clumsiness in getting dressed so soon after their minds were focused elsewhere delayed their escape from the enclosure, and they were still getting dressed by the time the Reverend had exited the Ferris Wheel, made his way to the "Salvation Station", unlocked the fastening securing the canvas walls of the tent, and taken Tilly inside where he was attempting to smooth out the wrinkles in her dress which had appeared across her bottom during the ride.

Elmer, in an attempt to give the lovers another minute or so to escape, walked around to the front of the tent to distract the Reverend a bit longer. Finding the flap open, he ducked in to find the Reverend rubbing Tilly's ass.

"Excuse me!" Elmer said.

"We won't be opening the tent to the public for another half hour," the reverend said, looking up from the task at hand.

"Well, I see my wife has volunteered to help you get everything set up so I thought I'd see if you needed my help as well."

"Oh, I see," said Reverend Goode, coming forward to shake Elmer's hand. "Yes, Mrs. Talbot generously agreed when I offered her the opportunity to help in the saving of those who have fallen into disrepute."

"She's remarkably pious!" Elmer asserted.

Before the conversation continued, Innocence came bouncing into the tent. "Hello daddy!" she said, giving him a hug. "Can I help?".

Gilt had apparently split for the moment.

"Sure, let's all get to work!" the Reverend directed.

Innocence returned to the site of her recent tryst, checking for any leftover clothing as she began bringing in the containers of merchandise. Elmer opened the containers, laying out the towels featuring Reverend Goode's picture on the merchandise table, including one towel he found on the shelf hidden under the pulpit. During this process, he discovered that his pocket was bulging due to the presence of Tilly's granny panties so left them on the shelf where the towel had been, intending to retrieve them later.

When everything was ready, it turned out that each of the three helpers had other plans that interfered with their ability to stay for the sermon and they left the Reverend to his work. This was too bad, because their absence caused them to miss the moment at the end when Reverend Goode reached down to the shelf under the pulpit to show off the holy towel he was offering for only $19.95 and inexplicably waved over his head a large pair of ladies undergarments!

~~~

8
TILLY AND ELMER – AND MARTHA

The annual South Branch High School "Labor Day Reunion Picnic" was in full swing, and by now most of the men had already consumed more than their minimum daily requirement of Bratwursts and Beer. Elmer and his old friend Eddie were reprising an argument that had begun the summer after they had graduated from high school, regarding which of them had caught the biggest fish on their last fishing expedition before leaving South Branch for college fifty years before. Neither could actually remember anything about the trip, except that it had occurred, but the argument had persisted for a half century.

Tilly interrupted the conversation. "Do you remember Martha Darling?"

"Now Tilly! You shouldn't call me 'darling' in front of Elmer, he might get suspicious!" Eddie averred.

Tilly laughed and gave Eddie a playful punch on his arm. "I'll be more careful next time 'Sweetheart'!" she said sweetly. "Martha Darling was in our class; don't you remember her? She was smart but rather shy."

"I guess I remember her a little," Elmer said. "I used to see her around school, but I don't remember ever having a conversation with her. Why?"

"We were casual friends in those days and she's just returned to South Branch from New York. She's a writer now and has just had a book published!"

"Good for her! Local girl makes good, huh? What's

the book about, Tilly?"

"I'm not sure. It's called 'Elmwood' but I don't know if that's a person or a place. I'm going to read it though!"

Tilly bought the book at Martha's book signing the next afternoon and began reading it after supper. She liked the book right away, and from time to time she was moved to read something aloud to Elmer:

" 'He caught me staring at him! Luckily, I was sitting on my bike at the time or my legs would have given out under me. This moment remains simultaneously the most exciting, and the most embarrassing, of my life. It was just a glimpse actually, and I turned away and pedaled as fast as I could back toward town, berating myself all the way for being in the wrong place at the wrong time, although I knew even then that I had been at exactly the RIGHT place at exactly the RIGHT time! I had never seen a boy naked before, and he looked breathtaking as he emerged from the swimming hole down at the creek.

'As I raced home, I tried to memorize every detail of him, even as I knew I would probably end up going to hell for my thoughts. Since my fate was sealed however, I thought I might as well concentrate on his most interesting and forbidden feature, and by the time I got home, I felt such a strange tingle between my legs that I had to touch myself there. It wasn't long before touching this forbidden spot became an obsession.' "

"Oh, it's that kind of book is it?" Elmer said.

"That's just the beginning Elmer! I can't wait to see what happens."

Tilly read late into the night, and then couldn't get

to sleep as she compared the story with events from her girlhood. Tilly found Martha's Book fascinating and somehow familiar.

"When I was near my secret lover, I rarely showed my face, instead observing him from a distance and trying to memorize his every feature and gesture, every facial expression and emotion. I eavesdropped on his conversations with his friends, even though I was in agony when he was talking with a girl who I was sure he was dating, or worse! I couldn't look at him without imagining him without clothes and I reviewed in my mind the details I could remember of his most outstanding body part.

"When I was alone in bed at night, however, my imagination filled in every detail that never happened in reality; he would gently undress me and then, when I was shivering with desire, he would tease me by undressing slowly before crawling under the covers. I could feel his warm bare skin against mine as we made love with my fingers standing in for his boyish manhood."

As Tilly and Martha rekindled their high school friendship, they began meeting for coffee during the afternoons at Pearl's Downtown Diner. The two had fun rehashing their school days and filling one another in on their comings and goings over the fifty years they had been in different parts of the country.

When the discussion turned to Martha's writing, Tilly was curious about where she got her ideas. Martha revealed that the story of Elmwood was primarily based on a boy she had known long ago. Having read the first third or so of the story, Tilly guessed correctly that Martha had known this boy when she was in high school which would mean that she probably knew him too. This redirected the conversation back to their adolescence and Tilly filled Martha in on what she knew of the whereabouts and accomplishments of the most popular of their classmates. Martha seemed especially interested in the endeavors of Buff Stevens, and this suggested to Tilly that Buff might have been the boy she had been writing about when she revealed her teenaged fantasies in her book. Due to Tilly's awkward meeting with Buff at their fiftieth class reunion, which Martha had not attended, she knew quite a bit of gossip about Buff, and this she recounted to Martha, pausing during the recounting, to inquire if Buff was the model for 'Elmwood". Martha just smiled and told her it would be best if the person she had been thinking of remained nameless.

That evening, Tilly took up her reading again, now especially curious as to the boy Martha had been writing about, and decided to elicit Elmer's help:

" 'As this little crush developed into a fixation, I found myself daydreaming about him, or trying to catch sight of him, every waking minute. In the evenings, I rode my bike past his house as often as I dared, wrote a VERY secret diary of imaginary things we had done together, and watched intently every lunchtime as he chatted in the hall outside the band room with the girl I imagined was his girlfriend. I was distraught with jealousy when I saw them together, but, at the same time, I was furious with her for seeming to be aloof when they were* *together. He needed a new girlfriend who would worship him, namely me, and I vaguely vowed to follow him forever in hopes that he would finally recognize that his true love was right here all along.' "*

"Who do you think she could be talking about, Elmer?"

"Me," he said as though the answer was obvious.

"YOU? Why would you think she had a crush on YOU!"

"Don't make it sound so impossible, Tilly! You had a crush on me after I let you grab my genitals on our first date!"

"Yes, but it was a date, Elmer! And, how many times do I have to remind you I never touched your genitals on our first date!"

"Well, she MIGHT have had a crush on me," Elmer said. "And she was kind of cute as I recall. Too bad I was wasting all my time on Suzibelle!"

"Well, Elmer, enjoy YOUR fantasy, but I think she had a crush on Buff Stevens."

"It couldn't have been Buff. He wasn't in the band and he never hung out outside the band room like I did."

Tilly considered this information but couldn't believe her rediscovered friend Martha had written a popular novel about an imaginary affair with her husband!

Tilly more or less avoided any probing into who the subject of Martha's novel might be at their next coffee get together, but the talk of the old days at South Branch

95

High continued. Martha studiously avoided asking any questions about Elmer, but she did seem unusually interested in Susan Belle's history and Tilly heard herself mention unintentionally that Elmer had had a crush on his "Suziebelle" before he and Tilly had gotten together. "I know!" Martha said.

As their meetings continued, and Tilly read further in the book, the idea that "Elmwood!" was based on Elmer began to sound less impossible. Tilly didn't really want to confront Martha about this possibility, but she was slightly concerned that if the story WAS based on true events, and Elmer WAS the boy Martha had been obsessed with, she might have returned to South Branch for another try at winning his heart!

Meanwhile, now that Elmer had become convinced that a popular novel had been written about him, he found himself unexpectedly interested in the book, and began reading Tilly's copy when she wasn't at home. This resulted in a rather nostalgic and revisionist remembrance of his high school days as they involved Martha Darling! He began to wonder why he had spent most of his time chasing hopelessly after his Suzibelle when Martha, who in his memory would have made a quite acceptable girlfriend, was following him around like a puppy without his noticing. Of course, it didn't take long for Elmer to migrate these thoughts to the present day and, completely without any encouragement on his part, he began picturing Martha inviting him along on her book signing tours to New York, Paris, and all the places where sophisticated readers were clamoring to see not only Martha, but the clueless boy she had written about. He tried to curtail this line of thought; what would Tilly say as he was globetrotting with a celebrity? Especially a celebrity who might very well not be able to resist the temptations of traveling with the boy she had been dreaming about for fifty years! He understood that this could cause a problem at home but, perhaps if he brought back armloads of jewelry from these exotic places, Tilly would understand it was just a business relationship between himself and the magnificent Martha.

To Tilly's annoyance, Elmer began finding excuses for going to town with her when she was having coffee with Martha, and he seemed to feel that it was fine for him to join them from time to time which, of course, eliminated the possibility of their discussing most of the more interesting topics on their agenda. His friendliness with Martha, coupled with Tilly's suspicions about the inspiration for her writing, made her even more concerned that this would all come to some kind of conflict eventually. Tilly wasn't terribly concerned that Elmer would fall for Martha or, heaven forbid, run off with her, but she didn't relish being compared to their celebrated jet setting former classmate, and if the word got out that the book was about Elmer, she didn't want to have to answer hundreds of questions about the situation from her friends and neighbors.

One Thursday afternoon, when Elmer was absent, Martha seemed unusually nervous when they got together.

"Tilly, I need to talk to you about something that may surprise you!" Martha said.

"Here it comes!" thought Tilly, taking a deep breath. "Oh?" she said cautiously.

"Tilly, I didn't come back for a long visit to South Branch only to promote my book!"

"You didn't?" she said.

"No. I came back to reconnect with someone who has been on my mind for quite some time."

Tilly was becoming increasingly concerned about what Martha was going to say and attempted to nip this in the bud. "Martha, you've been away for a half century and things aren't like they were in high school!"

"I know. This is awkward Tilly, but it's something I can't hide from you any longer. I hope you won't be upset, but even though it's been a long time, I've grown more and more fond of someone over the years, and I have feel I have to let them know in case they feel the same way about me!"

Tilly decided to lay her cards on the table before this went any further. "Martha, I know the book was about Elmer, but he and I have been married for nearly fifty years, and I'm not going to just let him go galivanting off with an old classmate!"

Martha smiled nervously. "Tilly, how far have you gotten in the book?"

"I've read all but the last chapter; enough to be sure it was about my husband!"

"You're right Tilly, the first eleven chapters of the

book WERE about Elmer. But when you read Chapter Twelve, that fact will be the last thing on your mind!"

Tilly couldn't imagine, now that Martha had acknowledged that the book was about Elmer, how that could be the last thing on her mind, and she was a bit concerned about what new information was about to be made known that would supersede her previous concerns.

"That must be quite a revealing chapter!" Tilly said. "You're making me a little uneasy about reading it!"

"Would you like me to read it to you?" Martha asked.

"I guess so," Tilly said.

"I'd like doing that, but I don't want to do it here in Pearl's Diner where others can hear us. How about if we walk over to the town square and find a quiet bench?"

"Ok."

The two women crossed the street to the town square, a park like block in the center of town that was the site of summer band concerts, occasional speechmaking, and a popular hangout for teenagers on warm summer nights. They arranged themselves facing each other on a park bench, and Martha once again expressed the hope that Tilly wouldn't be upset about what she was about to read. Tilly noticed in passing that Martha had arranged her crossed legs in a way that revealed she wasn't wearing anything under her skirt. This wasn't something that Tilly normally engaged in, but it was a hot day and Tilly assumed that this was probably the summer fashion among women from New York.

Martha smiled apprehensively at Tilly, took a deep breath, and began to read:

" 'Chapter 12 – Insight
'One morning, a few months after the breakup of my third marriage, I was preparing to move into a smaller but more elegant apartment in Manhattan. Among other things, this involved going through everything and eliminating any unnecessary memorabilia, especially as it related to the imperfect men in my life, which included all of them. This exercise was accompanied by an internal autobiography of my history with men and a somewhat self-indulgent assumption that I had, through no fault of my own, just chosen the wrong specimens. At this moment, I came across the 'Secret Diary' I had written as a schoolgirl about 'Elmwood' and our imaginary love affair. This should be interesting I thought, as I took a break from my categorization of paraphernalia and poured a generous ration of Scotch. As I read the imaginary diary, I noticed something surprising. I hadn't read this diary for fifty years, and whenever I thought of it, I assumed my thoughts centered on having scandalous sexual relations with 'Elmwood'. To my surprise, while nearly all of my fantasies involved the two of us in bed naked together, talking sweetly, holding each other close, and touching each other lovingly, there were very few entries where I wrote about being penetrated by any of his body parts, no matter how strange and interesting I had found them when I saw him at the creek. I thought at first that I might have been too shy or inexperienced to actually write about those fantasies, but that seemed unlikely since I was sure no one else*

would ever read this top-secret document!

'As I read, I began to realize that the fantasy relationship I had with Elmwood was not as related to his gender as it was to my enjoyment of affectionate closeness with someone. I took a mental detour through the relationships I've had with women over the years, and noticed that, in many cases, these relationships had been more satisfying than my relationships with men. I remembered wondering from time to time, what it would be like to have a sexual relationship with these women friends, but I just assumed that was out of the question since I wasn't gay. Now, as I considered this I wondered, for the first time consciously, whether my recurring marital problems might have been due to my choosing the wrong gender rather than the wrong male specimens.' "

Martha paused in her reading and looked at Tilly, who was busily processing this information but had yet to consider how it might have anything to do with her, apart from perhaps a bit of awkwardness when Martha introduced her to her most recent girlfriend.

"Shall I go on?" Martha asked.

"Of course!" Tilly said. "I can't wait to see where this is going!"

"I hope you like it when it gets there," Martha said.

"I stopped to ponder whether I wanted to follow this train of thought, but it was already clear to me where it was going, and I couldn't turn back. Had I been a lesbian all along and just failed to notice? Had I become a lesbian somewhere along the way and was only now discovering that fact? Or was this just an interesting idea but not really correct? I poured another glass

*of Scotch and began letting my thoughts follow their own flow
without trying to channel them into the familiar paths. As I
watched, almost like a third party, they returned to Elmwood
but now they began to focus on an image, almost certainly from
my high school days, of Elmwood at a swimming pool with a
friend and a teenaged girl dressed in a bathing suit. The young
girl was beautiful and was flirting with the two boys. Unseen
sparks of sexual arousal were flying back and forth between the
girl and Elmwood, and as I watched, some sparks also began
flowing between the girl and me. My thoughts began to focus on
the girl and how thrilling it was as the two of us silently
communicated our attraction to each other across the pool. By
now, this recalled, or imaginary, image was making my panties
wet. It was bedtime, so I finished my drink and got into bed, but
I couldn't sleep. In my imagination this girl and I held each other
and softly made love until I finally fell asleep, exhausted."*

Tilly was shocked! "Oh, my god, Martha! Were you
at the pool that day?"

"I don't know Tilly, do you remember an event like
that? I don't really remember it; I thought I had
imagined it!" Martha said. "Could it have really
happened?"

"I remember being at the city pool one afternoon just
before the beginning of our junior year," Tilly said. "I
was hanging out with Elmer and Eddie and I know I was
flirting with them like a nymphomaniac. I don't
remember seeing you specifically, but I was so horny
the vibes I was giving off might have caused radio static
all across the park!"

"Maybe it WAS real then! Anyway, Tilly, once I began to think I really should have fallen in love with a woman, YOU became that woman in my mind as I replayed what I thought was an imaginary experience in my mind."

The foreshadowing had somewhat prepared Tilly for the revelation that Martha was looking to hook up with another woman, but Tilly had not considered that SHE might be the person on Martha's mind, and was quite unprepared to respond. The two women looked at each other curiously and Tilly noticed that Martha had covertly moved her legs to hide her lack of panties.

Tilly didn't know what to say.

"I don't know what to say!" she said.

"You don't really have to say anything," Martha told her. "It's just something I needed to let you know. I'm not going to chase after you or anything. Unless you want me to of course!"

"Martha, I know it took a lot of courage for you to tell me and I feel you deserve a thoughtful response. I imagine you've been afraid I might have a VERY negative reaction, so you can relax on that, but as you probably expected, I'm mostly wired up the other way and now that I've got fifty or so years into training Elmer, I'm not thinking of ditching him for a romantic relationship with another woman."

"I understand, Tilly. Thanks for being straight with me, although your being 'straight' wasn't quite what I was hoping for."

"Have you experienced sex with another woman,

Martha?"

"Only in my imagination."

"I can give you some pointers if you like!" Tilly said.

"Tilly! Don't tell me you've done it with another woman!"

"You know I was in San Francisco during the summer of love, right?"

"Yes."

"Well, I didn't have any serious sexual relationships with any of my girlfriends, but we were very affectionate with each other and didn't think anything of teasing one another that way. It didn't make me gay, but it gave me an appreciation of the pleasures gay women could enjoy together."

"Tilly! You've given me an idea!"

"It sounds like you already had an idea!" Tilly laughed.

"This is a different idea. I'm going to start on a sequel to 'Elmwood'!"

"Oh, oh," Tilly said with a smile. "Do you have a title in mind?"

"I think 'Tiliaceous' would be good as a working title," Martha said.

"Does that word mean anything?" Tilly asked apprehensively.

"It's a species of tree, shady but fragrant, just like the main character. Maybe I'll just focus on writing about different kinds of trees from now on!" Martha said, giving Tilly's knee an affectionate squeeze.

~ ~ ~

9

ANNIVERSARY TEASE ON THE HIGH SEAS

Elmer closed his laptop.

"Ok, we're all set, Tilly! Sailing from Florida the end of September and returning on October 7th. Ports of call in Nassau, Cozumel, and Grand Cayman!"

"That will be perfect Elmer! Aren't you excited? Exactly the adventure we need to celebrate our Fiftieth Anniversary on the 5th!"

"I'm VERY excited!" Elmer said. "Seven romantic days at sea with my favorite person, being rocked to sleep by the ocean waves – after a little frolic! We might never get out of bed!"

"I'm afraid we'll have to eat sometimes, Elmer. And, according to the brochure, there are nine bars aboard, so we'll probably find something to do in between rolling around naked together like a young married couple!"

"I suppose we'll have to sip on a martini now and then to keep up our strength! Those olives are very healthy I'm told!"

"I can't wait to tell the kids, Elmer. They'll be so excited for us!"

As it turned out, the kids WERE very excited for mom and dad's romantic anniversary cruise; so excited that all of them decided it would be fun to celebrate with them! Sarah and Al signed on with Billy (7) and Beth (4). Their middle daughter Ellen, and her husband Rich, decided to join them with their three kids, Tommy (8), Judy (6), and Lucy (3), in tow. Making it unanimous, their son Ron and his latest girlfriend, Tammy, didn't want to miss out on the fun.

This news was received with mixed feelings; it would be fun to share the celebration with the family; and the five grandchildren would add a note of frivolity and excitement to the proceedings. On the other hand, it was clear that their offspring had no idea that mom and dad were anticipating plenty of private time together, a desire that Tilly and Elmer's progeny apparently thought their parents had outgrown years before.

"That will be fun, unless they expect us to babysit all the time!" Elmer said. "I hope we don't have adjoining rooms though! I don't want them listening to our cries of delight!"

"That would shock them!" laughed Tilly. "They'd probably think we were having a medical crisis or something!"

Their traveling companions booked cabins a few doors away from Tilly and Elmer's private hideaway and everyone was abuzz with anticipation. South Branch is a long way from the ocean, and Tilly and Elmer were looking forward to a high time on the high seas. Tilly focused her attention on updating her wardrobe with nautical themed attire: silky lingerie with sea life patterns, two new swimming suits just slightly too risqué for a woman her age, and slinky dresses to wear to dinner, even on casual nights. Elmer paid some uncharacteristic attention to his sartorial style as well, acquiring a mermaid themed tie and some brief silky briefs with comical seashell, swordfish, and octopus patterns applied in rather suggestive locations.

Tilly and Elmer studied the ship's itinerary and the assortment of available on-board activities. They planned to participate in a few of these, but the main focus of their sea going agenda was their desire to recapture the enchanted exhilaration of being together in their own secluded sea going sanctuary, far away from the familiar daily routine, where they could concentrate on each other as they had on their honeymoon. Naturally, they expected the carnal component of this concentration to be somewhat less frequent and less vigorous than fifty years before. But they knew it would be more skillfully carried out and no less prolonged or delightful. Being alone together in a strange and romantic place, with time to reminisce and celebrate their half century of marital escapades seemed like a perfect getaway. And a perfect excuse to fuck like they had just discovered the idea! Of course, in the interest of familial obligations, they would have to enjoy meals with the family once or twice a day, if they could manage to temporarily feign proper propriety.

Once on board, Tilly and Elmer toured the family's nearby accommodations and then retired to their quarters to get settled and prepare for the first big event, the "Bon Voyage Bash". They busied themselves kissing, discovering the amenities of their cabin, touching one another suggestively, unpacking their suitcases, and teasing one another about the details of their planned lovemaking marathon. In addition to their clothing, they had brought with them a number of playthings: three sculptural vibrating devices, two additional cylindrical toys, a generous container of "personal lubricant", and some other objects that they rarely used, but thought they should bring along just in case. These included various ropes, straps, and a leather object that they thought they might try one day for what is euphemistically called "impact play". They laid this assortment out on the bed and were in the process of deciding on the most appropriate hiding place for their sex toys when there was a commotion outside their door, accompanied by several children's voices demanding entry. Tilly and Elmer made funny frightened faces at each other, quickly pulled the bedspread over their collection, and let the five children in to inspect the old folks' quarters. Naturally, the children chose to begin their inspection by jumping on "Tutu" and "Emoo's" bed! This led to the discovery of various curious objects under the bedspread. These were unfamiliar to the children, who wanted an explanation; especially after Billy discovered that the bright pink one that looked kind of like a rocket began to vibrate when you pushed the button on the bottom!

Tilly demonstrated on each of the children that holding the object against the back of one's neck felt nice while Elmer quietly put the remaining contraband back into the suitcase, placed it on a high shelf in the closet, and then excitedly called the children to the large porthole to look at the dock workers who were using a fork-lift to move a truckload of food onto a lower deck of the ship.

"We'll be using a fork-lift ourselves when we see that food at dinner, won't we?" Elmer said to the children, only two of whom had any idea what he was talking about.

"Ok, shipmates," he ordered authoritatively. "Return to your quarters and prepare to set sail! Tutu and I will see you at the big party in a little while!"

The children loudly scrambled out while Elmer and Tilly smiled meaningfully at each other. "Good thinking

Tutu," Elmer said, squeezing her bottom.

The Bon Voyage party was fun with music, dancing, skits, and intoxicants for the grownups. This was followed by a lifeboat drill, a tour of the ship in which everyone but Ron and Tammy took part, and just enough time to dress up a bit for dinner. The clan gathered for a delightful meal, to which Ron and Tammy arrived a bit late. After lingering over dinner, the group then had just enough time to get to the evening stage show, a comic production which had enough razzmatazz to keep the children giggling and enough innuendo to entertain the adults.

Afterwards, Tilly and Elmer planned to enjoy a circumnavigation of the deck, perhaps stop at the bar specializing in Champagne for a celebratory libation, and then tuck in together and begin the opening ceremony of their anticipated week of reprising the undercover encounters of their original honeymoon. This scheme was delayed however, when Ellen suggested that Tilly and Elmer get together with the three young women to go over the list of shipboard activities and plan the week's events, while the dads took the children back to their cabins to do battle with the bedlam of bedtime. This motion carried although Tammy indicated she and Ron had plans for the evening but that they would be fine with whatever the others decided. Tilly and Elmer had ideas for the evening too, but they figured putting them off for a while would be all right; that would just intensify the passion of their planned assignation.

The planning committee met in Tilly and Elmer's room, opened a bottle of wine, and began the deliberations. The list of possible events was lengthy, and a major portion of the conversation involved the moms looking for activities to keep the children occupied while their parents enjoyed "private time" together in their cabins. Tilly and Elmer thought the concept of keeping the children out of mom and dad's hair should be applied to grownup children too but didn't mention it. More wine was consumed. The discussion evolved into gossip about the difficulties of parenting, and by the time the confab concluded, Tilly and Elmer were quite ready to tuck in together; which they did. And promptly fell asleep.

The next morning, bright sunlight shining through the large porthole of their room nudged Tilly and Elmer awake and they snuggled together, talking softly and touching one another in the teasing way they both loved. Unlike their younger days, when their libido routinely accelerated from zero to sixty in 3.2 seconds, these days they could enjoy a leisurely lead-in to the lollygagging, and this was delightfully under way when the bedside phone rang.

"Up and at 'em, Tutu and Emoo! The children are coming down to your room in a few minutes to escort you to breakfast! We have lots of exciting things to do today, time to look bright eyed and bushy tailed!"

Tilly and Elmer looked at each other, noted that they only had one exciting thing on THEIR schedule, and then got up so as to be dressed when the children arrived.

The days on board ship began to follow a pattern that seemed perfectly contrived to sabotage Tilly and Elmer's sought-after solitude. They didn't want to miss meals with the family, especially as they anticipated the amusing antics of the children, and times between meals were filled with watching the kids showing off their newly gained swimming skills, as well as reading, sitting in the sun, shopping for souvenirs, and spontaneously stopping for a casual cocktail with one or two of their adult children. Of course, they also wanted to be involved in the general buzz of shipboard excitement.

One afternoon, Tilly and Elmer were determined to slip away to their cabin for a rendezvous, but even this was waylaid by the unexpected discovery that the children had learned how to use their cabin's telephone to call Tutu and Emoo's room. The grandchildren thought this was a fun way to invite themselves over, or to invite the grandparents to come and applaud their latest art project, cooking success, or swimming achievement. Evenings were often spent in pleasant conversation with the family, which they didn't want to miss either.

In contrast to Tilly and Elmer's somewhat frustrating inability to avoid excess popularity, Ron and Tammy rarely left their cabin and, when they did participate in family gatherings, they usually looked distracted and disheveled. And delighted! Tilly and Elmer were somewhat envious of their single mindedness, but assured each other that the excess family togetherness would wear off after a few days and that by the date of their actual anniversary, October 5th, they could spend the entire day giggling and chasing each other around their quarters, not to mention catching each other from time to time.

They should have known better.

They began the big day snuggling in bed together and engaging in an amusing argument over how many times they had made love on their wedding night fifty years earlier. As Elmer was working out a rough calculation in his mind about approximately how many times they had done it in fifty years of marriage, and a few years of practice before then, Tilly noticed that a red light was blinking on their bedside phone, an indication of a waiting message. She picked up the phone to discover that the message was a reminder that she and Elmer had a reservation for a couple's massage at 10 AM, just after breakfast!

"Did you book a massage for us at 10, Elmer?" she asked.

"I intend to be massaging you long before that!" Elmer informed her.

"No, I mean an official 'couple's massage'?"

"No, where did you get that idea?"

"That's what the message was about. It must be a mistake. I'll let them know," Tilly said, picking up the phone. Elmer listened to Tilly's half of the conversation.

"Oh, they did? Isn't that sweet? We'll see you at 10 then! Thank you! Guess what Elmer! Our children booked a couple's massage for us at 10, right after breakfast! Wasn't that nice of them?"

"I booked a couple's massage for us at – let's see – right now!" Elmer chuckled. "And we don't even have to get out of bed!"

"We'll have time for that later Elmer. For now, we'd better go meet them for breakfast and thank them!"

The couple's massage was lovely and by the time they were finished and fully relaxed, it was time for lunch. Everyone was in attendance this time, and Tilly and Elmer were embarrassed but amused by the staff who serenaded their fiftieth anniversary with songs, funny hats, and a parade around the dining room during which Tilly and Elmer were seated on an elaborate cart and pushed around like they had just won the World Series. They were even more self-conscious during the "interview" where they were asked the secret of staying married to the same person for a half century. Elmer had a notion to tell the unwitting onlookers scandalous secrets of their sex life, but he thought Tilly would prefer that he be slightly more discrete, so he just said, "Choose the cutest girl in town and get lucky!"

Of course, this revelation was greeted by their fellow diners with laughter and nodding of heads and Tilly and Elmer were released from their celebrity status with cheers and good wishes. After this excitement, the lovers decided to skip dessert and go back to their cabin for a "nap". Before they could make their excuses however, the grandchildren let them know that their attendance was expected at the afternoon presentation of "The Tale of the Troublesome Treasure!", as performed by the "Midship Players". This was mandatory of course, especially since the two oldest grandchildren had leading roles (as did a dozen or so of their fellow thespians). Tilly gave Elmer a covert poke in the ribs as it became clear that the premise of the play involved a group of pirates who knew the location of the hidden treasure but suffered multiple setbacks in their attempts to snatch it!

"Just like us!" Elmer responded in a whisper.

One thing led to another and, after a backstage tour, ice cream to celebrate the successful performance, and a treasure hunt around the ship revealing secret places and mysterious doorways the kids had found in their travels, it was nearing time for dinner. Tilly and Elmer returned to their cabin to get dressed for the special dinner the grownups had planned in one of the exclusively fancy restaurants on board. The showering and dressing proceeded slowly and was primarily slow-motion foreplay; fun even though they were well aware that they wouldn't have time to carry out their full agenda of bodily frivolity before the evening fete. Nevertheless, they helped each other get dressed, commenting positively on each other's appearance in and out of their clothing, and going out of their way to smooth imaginary wrinkles in one another's garments once they had put them on.

The dinner was lovely and featured a special bottle of expensive champagne and a dessert festooned with minor fireworks and congratulatory messages. Even Rob and Tammy stayed for the entire event, although they couldn't keep their hands off each other and, in a naughty and playful mood, Tilly and Elmer raised a few eyebrows themselves with some mild public displays of affection. Of course, they had to put up with some teasing over this and when Rob suggested they "get a room" they giggled that they had a room, they just hadn't had time to make use of it.

After dinner, it was revealed that the adult children had brought along anniversary gifts for the happy couple and that a small after-dinner party would be convening in Ellen and Rich's cabin now that dinner was over. Since it was to be a grownup party, the children were put to bed in Tilly and Elmer's room, with a baby monitor nearby to be sure all was well, and the celebrants gathered for a continuation of the evening's festivities. The grownup children maneuvered Tilly and Elmer into a recounting of their early life together and teased the stories of a few previously unknown naughty misadventures out of them. Tilly and Elmer were a bit tipsy, but not so sloshed as to give away too many ancient secrets, and they were determined to get to bed before they were too tired to finally carry out their number one cruise agenda on date of their anniversary.

They said their goodnights, invited the children to retrieve the sleeping grandkids from their room, and prepared to tuck in for the culmination of their anniversary celebration.

"Remember how desperate for one another we used to get back when we were just married?" Tilly asked. "I remember when we hadn't done it for a while, we would be so ready we'd start undressing each other before we even got to our room!"

She accompanied this inquiry by beginning to pull his shirttail out of his pants with one hand and to loosen his tie with the other, as they were walking back to their cabin. Elmer responded by giving her a pat on the butt and then grasping the zipper that closed the rear of her dress at the top and began to slowly inch it down. When Tilly complained that anyone making their way down the corridor behind them could observe his too public tomfoolery, he fell into place behind her, both to hide his activity and to gain easier access to her zipper. Fortunately for the preservation of shipboard propriety, they reached their cabin just as Elmer was about to unfasten the now exposed back of her bra and he accomplished this task just as they closed their cabin door.

In their younger days, the removal of one another's clothing was accomplished as quickly as possible since at that time they considered each other's garments as merely an obstacle to getting started on the main event. Their lovemaking was chaotic and wild, and an onlooker could have described it as pugilistic as easily as lustful. Now their romantic assignations were as beautiful as ballet – choreographed but improvised; rhythmic but random. Every sense was satisfied, every request fulfilled even if unspoken. Many requests WERE spoken though! An ongoing joke at this point was that their hearing required sweet nothings to be shouted rather than whispered.

Inside their seagoing love nest, they took their time undressing and fondling each other in front of the large round porthole as they looked at the last of the sunset and the rhythmic sparkle of the rising moon on the waves. They were very aware that this was an unusually special moment; the fiftieth anniversary of their marriage, their first romantic cruise together, traveling away from home in a beautiful and unfamiliar place, not to mention that they had just experienced a period of unintended abstinence. Their lovemaking was always good, but this was going to be the best yet. They both, without having a conversation about the moment, resolved to make this night perfect.

Elmer regarded Tilly's body. He had deliberately removed her underthings, leaving her dressed only in her silky light-colored dress, which glowed around the outline of her nude body within as it was silhouetted in the moonlight. Tilly had removed Elmer's clothing, except for his briefs and socks, and had loosely retied his tie so it hung down over his bare chest. He looked silly and beautiful. They danced without music, and then carefully sprawled across the bed together and awkwardly rolled around softly kissing whichever body part they came in contact with. They began making love slowly and sensuously, softly touching the areas that each knew would drive the other wild and turn up the flame under their growing desire.

Elmer whispered to Tilly how fifty years of marriage had only enhanced her beauty in his eyes. Tilly, in a moment of passion, giggled and loudly told him how she loved his cock, which Elmer immediately offered to share with her!

They expertly maneuvered their bodies into a comfortable position for coupling, then slowly and luxuriously took turns bringing each other to a glorious climax. Once they had recovered a bit, they lay quietly together, celebrating their skill at that activity and their pleasure in the fact that making love together, while different than when they were newlyweds, was still as delightful as ever. Finally, they allowed the rocking of the vessel and the music of the engines below to help them drift off to sleep. Just before she finally nodded off, Tilly became aware of a small green light that seemed to come from the bedside table, but, assuming it was just another of their collection of electronic devices, she resolved to check on its source in the morning.

Their evening's exertion and the rocking of the boat conspired to cause them to sleep like babies, and when they finally woke up in the morning, they found they didn't have time for a post-coital snuggle as that would make them late for breakfast. They kissed sweetly, then got up and begin to prepare for their last full day at sea. As they were leaving their room, Tilly remembered the curious light she had seen just before falling asleep and stopped to locate its source.

"Oh, oh, Elmer!" she said.

"Oh, oh, what, sweetheart?" Elmer asked.

"I saw a little light on something by the bed last night just before I fell asleep, now I see what it was!"

"What?"

"A baby monitor!"

"Oops! You don't suppose they left the baby monitor

in our room last night, do you?"

"Well, it got there somehow. Maybe they turned it off after they took the children back to bed!"

"We hope!" Elmer said, grinning and giving her a kiss.

When they arrived at breakfast, a little late, nothing was said about any listening in on their evening's activities, although their grownup children did seem to be trying to avoid any conversation even vaguely related to the previous evening.

Tilly and Elmer began to relax and assume their frisky frolic from the previous evening had not been accidently revealed. And anyway, the little ones would have been asleep, so even if the grownups heard something, they should have expected that mom and dad were not heading back to their cabin to go right to sleep on their fiftieth anniversary. Until Billy spoke up:

"Tutu, did you and Emoo have a chicken in your room?"

"A chicken?" Tilly said.

"Yes! I heard you say you loved Emoo's cock, and he said you could share it!"

The younger children were quite curious about how, and why, their grandparents would smuggle a chicken onto the ship, and the grownups were either pale or red faced as they tried to cover up the fact that they had been listening over the baby monitor, and simultaneously concoct a plausible explanation that would satisfy the children without revealing anything. Tilly and Elmer looked at their offspring for a minute as they let them wrestle with this complicated dilemma that required a quick answer. Sarah's attempted explanation to the children, that it involved something that was only for grownups, didn't satisfy the questioners in the slightest.

Finally, Elmer gave the grownup children a look and explained the situation:

"You know that grownups sometimes drink alcohol, and it's all right for grownups now and then, but it isn't all right for children, don't you?"

"Yes, the children agreed."

"And you know that some kinds of alcohol are called cocktails, right?"

"Yes."

"So, in this case, a 'cock' didn't mean a chicken, it was a nickname for 'cocktail'. Tutu wanted to taste my cocktail and I agreed. It tasted good too, didn't it Tilly?"

"It was delicious, Emoo!" she said.

This resolved the problem for the moment, and there was no further discussion with the children, grownup or not, as Tilly and Elmer expected. Their adult children eventually got their just deserts however when, at their next dinner party, the little children inquired in front of the guests whether everyone was going to have a cock before dinner.

~~~

10
TILLY AND ELMER'S OLD HAUNTS

"Guess what we're going to be doing on Halloween, Tilly!"

"Watching TV as usual?"

"Not this year! I'll give you a hint. It will bring back memories!"

"Good ones, or bad ones?"

"Probably mixed," Elmer chuckled. "It does involve kissing though, so that's good!"

"Are we going to get dressed up and reprise our first kiss outside on the porch?"

Elmer raised an eyebrow. "I'd go for that as long as you promise not to push me down the front steps like you did fifty-eight years ago!"

"To begin with, you know I never pushed you down the front steps – I only knocked you on your ass!" Tilly laughed.

"Ok, I'll risk the kiss," Elmer said. "But first, we're going to the high school dance like we did in 1961!"

"And what will we be doing at a high school dance may I ask?"

"Our friend Al is in charge of finding chaperones for the Halloween dance at South Branch High this year. Most of the faculty have 'other plans' so he's looking for old alums to keep the lovesick young couples in line. It should be a kick!"

"It sounds like a very scary way to spend Halloween!" Tilly said. "How about we just watch a horror movie on TV? I'll pretend to be scared and then we can get into bed and you can comfort me!"

"I'll comfort you afterward. But the dance will be fun, and you don't have to worry about me stepping on your feet like I did back then!"

Tilly considered the proposition. "Will we be in costume?" she asked.

"I think we should reprise our costumes from 1961! I can do my fantastic pirate costume and you can don your dramatic Dracula duds!"

"Don't forget I was a cute Dutch country girl from the neck down, Elmer. You never really understood that costume, did you?"

"I understood it enough to fall hopelessly in love with you while you were wearing it. Of course, I fell for the kiss more than the costume."

"You weren't too hot for the fangs either, as I recall!" Tilly observed.

"No, I didn't fall in love with you until you took them out!"

Tilly and Elmer did their best to recreate their decades old costumes from junior year and arrived at the dance at the appointed time. They were surprised to find the school gym decorated almost exactly as it had been for the 1961 Halloween dance! As before, the gym was entered through a door decorated to suggest a huge mouth with cardboard fangs along each side and with two squinty eyes crowded into the wall space above the door. Inside, a few pumpkins and cornstalks symbolized the slow pace of change in South Branch since they were essentially identical to the ones Elmer and Tilly had encountered as high school juniors.

The changes were concentrated in the attendees! For one thing, attendance was lower than when they were students and it seemed most of the revelers came as part of small groups rather than with a "date". Tilly and Elmer were also surprised that the costumes, unlike the elaborate and imaginative regalia they remembered, consisted largely of street clothes, jeans for the guys, shorts and tights for the young women, accented by a scarf, necklace, or amusing hat or wig. Nothing scary in sight.

"No fangs either! All the better for kissing!" Elmer mused to himself.

In addition to the fact that there was little in the way of scary costumes, there was little in the way of dancing either. Of course, Tilly and Elmer hadn't paid any attention to popular music for approximately forty years, so the meaning of the melodies was lost on them. And the dancing consisted primarily of a crowd of people jumping up and down with no way to tell if anyone was dancing "with" anyone else. It didn't seem very sexy to Tilly and Elmer, but they didn't find this shortcoming objectionable.

"How OLD have we become, Tilly?" Elmer wondered. "We're looking at these young people just like the chaperones looked at US fifty-eight years ago!"

"They do seem to have a different mindset than we did though, Elmer," Tilly shouted over the music. "But they probably are still going to be kissing after the dance is over. Quite possibly more than just kissing!"

"I hope it doesn't take them a year after the kiss to move on to going all the way," Elmer said, although from his current point of view his thoughts on this subject had become a bit more conservative than they had been a half century before.

As they observed the young people and contemplated how confident and capable they seemed, compared to how clumsy they had been at that age, Tilly and Elmer noticed another big difference in the current dance scene. Everyone seemed to spend most of their time looking at their cell phones and texting.

"If their friends are here," Elmer wondered, "Who could they be sending all those texts to?"

"They're probably sending photos of what's happening on THIS side of the gym to their friends on the OTHER side!" Tilly suggested.

The bleachers were in place along one side of the gym, and Tilly and Elmer perched a few rows up so that they could survey the scene as well as keep out of the way of the menacing mass of bouncing dancers.

"Aren't they all so cute!" Tilly asked, putting her arm around Elmer and beginning to tear up a little at how awkward they had been at their first dance together, and how miraculous it suddenly seemed that they were back here, still together nearly sixty years later. She put her fingers on Elmer's chin, turned his face toward hers, and gave him a romantic kiss.

In spite of the difference in high school dance culture

since they attended as students, the atmosphere of young love was omnipresent and this stirred up, in Tilly and Elmer, sweet memories of those days when they couldn't think of anything but each other. Before long they began touching each other affectionately, ignoring the bouncing dancers below.

Suddenly, Tilly began to laugh hysterically.

"What's so funny?" Elmer inquired.

"Remember the PDA monitors, Elmer? Not that we ever had occasion to run afoul of their prurient presence."

In earlier times, the dances were monitored by roving groups of voyeuristic grown-ups whose task it was to warn couples who were too obviously fond of each other against PDA, "Public Displays of Affection".

"It was just as well that we preferred to display our affection in private!" Elmer noted.

It was the custom during earlier times for most couples to stay until the dance ended, but groups and couples began drifting away earlier and Tilly and Elmer were assigned to the parking area to be sure there were no troublesome incidents. They retired to Elmer's truck and watched as groups emerged from the building, broke up into cars, and left for other venues. No one was observed being picked up by his or her parents!

Some of the departing dancers remained in their cars and, to Tilly and Elmer's amusement, they seemed to be engaging in displays of affection that were, conveniently, at least partially concealed in the darkened vehicles. On occasion, they heard giggling or scary screaming, which was obviously caused by adolescent Halloween hijinks. They didn't have much chaperoning to do, but they stayed at their post in the truck for voyeuristic as well as nostalgic reasons.

Tilly's costume consisted of a rather short skirt with a plain white blouse suggesting the clothing of a young Dutch country girl, while Elmer's pirate costume consisted of shorts, a dark shirt with the sleeves rolled up and the top buttons undone, finished off with a red bandana. The aura of young romance and their current situation, sitting close together in a dark vehicle, made both of them nostalgic for their intense high school love affair, and they involuntarily began kissing sweetly. Tilly placed her hand on Elmer's thigh and teased him lovingly. This gesture had stimulated Elmer in a particular way since she had first done this by accident on their first date, and it aroused him the same way this time. Nothing seemed amiss among the remaining cars, many of them occupied by loving couples, so Tilly and Elmer continued to pass the time in teasing each other in a way that would have been referred to as "necking" in their younger days. They began discussing the circumstances and awkwardness of their first kiss fifty-eight years before, and when Elmer recounted that Tilly had asserted at the time, as he was feeling terminally stupid about his clumsy first attempt to kiss her, that they would be laughing about that moment fifty years in the future, he fell in love with her all over again. They began complimenting each other on their lovable qualities and their hands began touching each other's most sensitive body parts under their clothing. Naturally, the need to navigate around unnecessary garments to twiddle each other led to the removal of the offending items and eventually, they were nearly naked in the love nest that the '53 Chevy pickup had become once again.

They had learned the hard way over the last few years that any attempt to engage in traditional sexual intercourse in the confines of this conveyance could cause severe muscular distress over the following week, so they fell into a delightful dalliance consisting of rhythmic manipulation of one another's genitalia and, especially as they remembered the beneficial effect this had on them during their high school courtship, the ardor of their activities grew to suppress any notice of their location or of any activities occurring in the surrounding countryside.

Tilly, who had never been a Boy Scout but was nevertheless known for always being prepared, kept a small personal vibrator in her purse. She had a hard time imagining the exact situation where this would be required, but she assumed such a situation night arise; and now it had! Elmer's expert ministrations were beautiful, but occasionally Tilly liked a bit of a buzz to boost her to the pinnacle of pleasure. This vibrating device could be attached to one's finger, and she gave Elmer a long kiss and slipped it around the finger he was manipulating her with as a subtle suggestion. By now the necking had evolved into foreplay, at least foreplay foreshadowing a frenzy of frigging one another with their fingers. Elmer turned on the vibrator, which in turn, turned on Tilly. The fact that they had spent a significant portion of their high school careers engaging in this same activity in the same vehicle gave the evening a familiar feeling as did their manipulative activities, and they were happily anticipating a familiar outcome to the proceedings. Their teasing was on a trajectory to bring Tilly to a shivery and vocal orgasm momentarily whereupon, once she had recovered her wits, she would cause Elmer to express his pleasure in the usual way.

For now, the interior of the truck was quiet except for the humming of Tilly's vibrator and her occasional sounds of satisfaction or suggestions for the minor repositioning of her delight producing device. These minor background noises masked a similar humming sound from behind them that would soon bring an unexpected climax to Tilly and Elmer's Halloween tryst in the truck!

Due to decades of careful research, Elmer was the world's greatest expert in gauging how close Tilly was to reaching the apogee of her arousal and he could tell by her rapid breathing, quivering muscles, and the urgency with which she squeezed his forearm that she was just about there. A moment later, Tilly screamed "Oh My God" and hugged him, desperately pressing her face into his chest. This was dramatic but an unusual response, compared to her customary climactic culmination. Nevertheless, Elmer at first thought that he had handled his ministrations with even more skill than usual and was congratulating himself when Tilly screamed, "WHAT WAS THAT?"

"What?" Elmer asked.

"Outside!" she said, her face still hidden against his chest.

Elmer looked up and saw what Tilly was talking about. His jaw dropped, but he had no answer to Tilly's question.

A ghostly figure was hovering in midair just beyond the front windshield of the truck. It was the size of a small person, but it consisted of waving, semitransparent tentacles which glowed intermittently with a ghoulish red color. Strangely, the entire interior of the truck was illuminated with a similarly pulsing red light, and there was an unusual humming sound in the air.

Elmer was not a believer in ghosts, even on Halloween, but he could not come up with an explanation for the strange object that was alternately moving away and then back toward them. His immediate response to this unnerving and unexplained phenomenon was to get out of there as soon as possible. Carrying out their escape took longer than he hoped however, because he had to first untangle himself from his mostly naked and somewhat hysterical wife, then awkwardly remove his shorts and briefs which were wrapped around his ankles, preventing him from operating the vehicle. Finally, he could move his limbs sufficiently to drive, found the keys in the pocket of his wayward shorts, started the truck, and accelerated toward the exit of the parking area. The ghostly object only followed them for a short distance, but the pulsing red light continued to illuminate the truck's interior. Elmer located the source of this annoyance when he looked in the rear-view mirror to see the red lights atop a police car following them. He didn't think they had done anything illegal, but Tilly was curled up on the seat beside him, unmoving, clad solely in an unbuttoned blouse and white bobby socks, and he was naked from the waist down since he had not taken the time to reinstall his shorts after untangling them.

The situation looked scary!

Elmer drove carefully toward the exit, taking care not to do anything that might be illegal. Once they had exited the parking lot and had reached the main road, the police car was no longer behind him and gradually their breathing returned to normal. Tilly retrieved her garments and put on a couple of the most crucial ones. Once they arrived at home, and were parked in their driveway, they redistributed their clothing around the interior of the truck and took up where they had left off. This time, they both reached outstanding orgasms without being undone by UFO's, witches, or trick or treating pranksters.

Several days went by, and they were still stumped by the curious object they had seen. Then they received a package from Elmer's old friend Eddie, who was at this point, South Branch's assistant chief of Police:

South Branch Police Department
Edward Berins, Assistant Chief

Dear Elmer and Tilly,

Thought you'd like to know what that was over your truck in the South Branch High parking lot Halloween night, and by the way, that was me following you on the way out! We had a call about some high school kids who had dressed a drone up in a "skirt" to vaguely resemble a ghostly jellyfish and were using it to scare other kids after the dance. As you may know, it's against the law to fly drones on the high school grounds when a school activity is under way, so this device was confiscated. You may also know that drones typically have video cameras in them, and you'll never guess what we found when we downloaded the video from the flight over your '53 Pickup! Well, I'm sure you CAN guess, but I thought it would be thoughtful to send you the only copy of the video so no one else will know what unimaginable improprieties you and Tilly were up to on Halloween night. Except Meg and me of course!

Happy Halloween (apparently),
Eddie

~~~

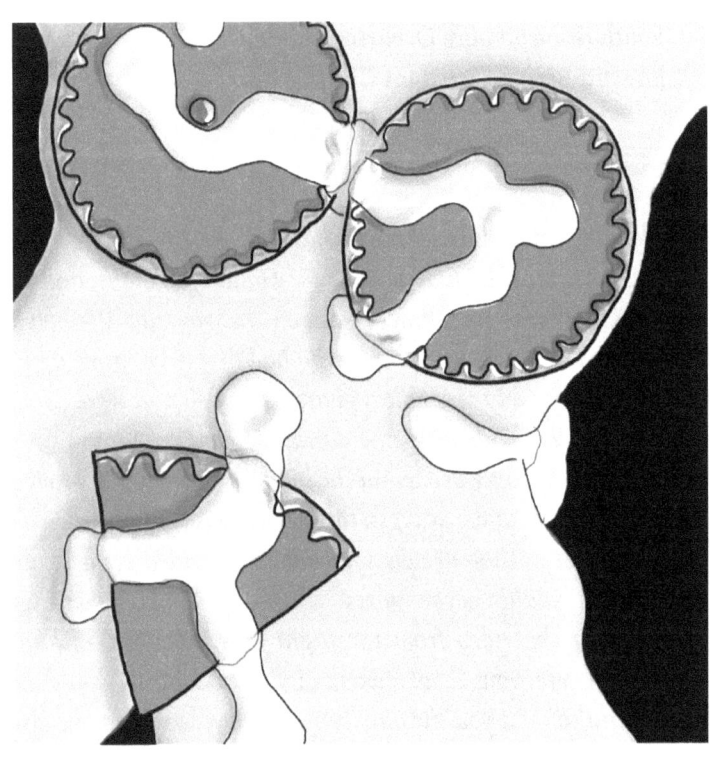

11
AN UNSEEMLY SCENE WITH WARM WHIPPED CREAM

Elmer slowly became aware of large figure floating in midair above him; a large, soft, unclothed female figure, who smiled down and seemed to be wordlessly communicating to him. To his surprise, she seemed to be suggesting that they enjoy a sexual romp together, a suggestion that he found thrilling and remarkably arousing, although his delight was counterbalanced by his vague understanding that Tilly would not be happy if he followed through on this seemingly reasonable and harmless suggestion. As he struggled with this temptation, the figure gradually morphed into the shape of an elephant, which he recognized as Dumbo. This was both a major disappointment and something of a relief, since now he didn't have to decide how to manage this awkward choice.

He heard a distant voice, which he came to realize belonged to Tilly, saying, "Elmer! Are you ready to wake up and start fucking?"

Elmer's gradually awakening brain parsed this question, and he sleepily replied in the affirmative.

"Good! Wake up and let's get started in the kitchen!"

Elmer wasn't sure he had heard Tilly correctly. "You want to fuck in the kitchen?" he asked slowly.

"Elmer! I want you to get up and help me COOK in the kitchen. You know Sarah and Al will be here tomorrow morning and we have lots to do, starting with the pumpkin pies."

Elmer wrangled his thoughts away from the huge, affectionate, naked woman who had turned into Dumbo – he must have been dreaming about the Thanksgiving Day parade from New York – and found himself mostly awake, although a little sad that the huge woman wasn't really going to float down and smother him with affection. Not yet fully awake, Elmer muttered, "I love fat women!"

"Well, you may get your wish after tomorrow, Elmer!" Tilly said. "It always takes me weeks to lose the weight I gain on Thanksgiving!"

Elmer gradually realized that he was now mostly awake. He had a vague concern that something had just gone on between himself and Tilly that she wasn't going to be happy about, but she was already up and on the way to the shower.

"I still love her ass!" he thought, admiring her progress toward the bathroom.

Thanksgiving had, in recent years, involved their daughter Sarah and her husband Al driving down from Des Moines with their two children, Billy and Beth. As a result, the day before Thanksgiving was usually given over to cooking, overindulging in intoxicants, and giving thanks for their continued affection for one another by means of some kind of playfully uninhibited physical indulgence.

Elmer was still in bed as Tilly got out of the shower, affording him another opportunity to give thanks for the shape of her body. True, she wasn't eighteen anymore, but she still turned him on. He loved the soft, rounded shape she had grown into. The fact that gravity seemed to have influenced the distribution of some of her most charming parts didn't detract from her beauty in his mind. Beyond her physical attractiveness, her smile, sass, and playful personality still made him feel thankful for his good luck, and not only on Thanksgiving.

"I know you'd like to spend the rest of the day in bed gazing at my fabulous naked body as I sashay around the bedroom teasing you, but we really need to get started on the pumpkin pies. And, Elmer, the sooner we get them finished the sooner we can get started on demonstrating how thankful we are to be together!"

This reminder convinced Elmer to get out of bed. He spent a few minutes in the bathroom, and when he got to the kitchen, Tilly was beginning the cooking. As a further incentive to get going on the work, Tilly was wearing only an apron. Of course, this was as much a distraction as it was an inducement, so it didn't really speed up the process.

"Ok, Tilly. What do I do first?" he said, softly sliding his palm across her bottom.

"Start by washing your hands," she laughed, "while I get out the ingredients for the crust!"

Tilly measured out the flour and put it into a large bowl, finishing by dipping her fingers into the bowl and flicking a small dusting of flour on to Elmer's bare chest.

"Elmer, take these cold sticks of butter and cut them up into half inch cubes. Then dump them in with the flour!"

Elmer obeyed her instructions without question.

Tilly added salt and began using a pastry cutter to cut the butter into small grains and mix it in with the flour. Elmer, clad only in black boxers, stood behind her, looking over her shoulder and carefully observing the process while he reached around under her apron and massaged her breasts.

"Quit messing around and go get the vodka," she instructed.

"That sounds like 'messing around' to me!" Elmer chuckled. "Are we taking a much-needed break from our cooking project?"

"The vodka is going into the pie crust, Elmer. But I suppose we could sample a little to be sure it's still good. We don't want to put bad vodka in our special pie crust, and anyway 8:30 in the morning isn't really THAT early!"

Tilly mixed the ice-cold vodka with an equal amount of cold water and added it to the bowl, while Elmer poured equal measures of vodka and orange juice into two small glasses. The dough was rolled into a ball, then cut in half and partially flattened into two rounds that went into the refrigerator to cool.

"Here's to a healthy breakfast," Elmer said, as they toasted their pie progress.

It was snowing outside, with big, soft, fluffy, flakes falling lazily past the kitchen window. Tilly and Elmer stood at the sink, sipping their breakfast vodka and quietly giving thanks that they were indoors. Tilly's apron was tied in the back, which left her entire backside exposed, so Elmer took advantage of the opportunity to gently rub her bare bottom. Since they had an hour or so to wait for the dough to cool before they needed to start on the pie filling, Elmer built a fire in the living room fireplace and turned the sofa to face the hearth. Tilly joined him and they sat on the floor, leaning back against the front of the sofa to wait for part two of their cooking project. They snuggled together in front of the warm fire, touching one another and laughing about some of their previous Thanksgiving mishaps. A few of these involved cooking failures, but before they had children underfoot, and after the children had left home, the mishaps were more likely to be the product of a problematic but tasty proposal to add pumpkin pie or whipped cream to their sexy shenanigans.

"We used to find a number of desirable uses for pumpkin pie in our kinky romps, didn't we?" Elmer asked rhetorically.

"Yes we did, Elmer," Tilly said. "And as good as pumpkin pie is when eaten from a plate, it's even better when it's licked off a warm body!" She kissed his warm belly.

"Especially with whipped cream!" Elmer agreed. "Maybe we should make an extra pie just in case!"

"Don't you think we're getting a little too old for that kind of foolishness?" Tilly asked.

"If I ever get too feeble to nibble whipped cream off

your nipples, you have permission to put me out to pasture," Elmer asserted, as Tilly felt a little shiver of pleasure at the memory of how much she enjoyed that uncommon activity.

Tilly got up and went into the kitchen for a minute, returning with the bottles of orange juice and vodka. While she refilled their glasses, Elmer pulled the cushions off the sofa and built a small nest on the floor into which they snuggled, sitting facing each other and wrapping their legs around each other's hips. This led to manual teasing and, combined with the drinks, the warm fire, and the snowy weather, put them into a lovely amorous mood.

Some time passed. In fact, a lot of time passed.

Eventually, Tilly checked the time. "Everything should be more than chilled enough that we can start on the filling now, Elmer," she announced, reluctantly untangling her legs from Elmer's and getting up with a groan.

Elmer followed her into the kitchen. "Ok Tilly, what do we do next?"

"You can crack the eggs and put them into this bowl."

Tilly added the brown sugar and the necessary amount of canned pumpkin to the eggs and set Elmer to the task of whipping them into a mixture. When he finished, she added an array of other ingredients: spices, cream, cornstarch, and more, whereupon Elmer whipped this mixture to the proper consistency.

Tilly took charge of the rounds of dough, shaped

them, and put the crusts in the oven to pre-bake. While the baking was taking place, Tilly whipped up a small amount of whipped cream.

"Are you sure that will be enough?" Elmer asked.

"We'll have to make more tomorrow before we serve the dessert," Tilly told him.

"I know Tilly, but will it last us through the next hour or two of wicked licking?"

"If it doesn't, we'll think of something else to lick off each other," she said, leading Elmer back to the living room floor.

Their increasing silliness was interrupted when the kitchen timer went off. Tilly went into the kitchen to add the filling, then returned the pies to the oven. When Tilly rejoined Elmer by the fire she had left her apron behind and the silliness resumed by the fireplace.

Elmer pointed out to Tilly how much he still loved the shape of her breasts.

"They used to be pretty nice, didn't they, Elmer? Too bad they're all saggy these days!"

"I don't get why women's breasts that have a few miles on them would be considered inferior to when they were new," Elmer said. "They are still beautifully round and soft. Not only that but they are exactly the right size. As we used to say when we were boys, 'Anything more than a handful is just wasted'!"

"I'm glad you still like them, Elmer," Tilly giggled. "You may show them your fondness for fondling them if you wish!"

Elmer was an expert at this activity, the world's greatest expert as far as Tilly was able to determine, and her titties were totally titillated as usual when be began demonstrating his dexterity. Tilly leaned back against Elmer's chest as they sat against the front of the sofa facing the fire. Elmer gathered a breast in each hand and tenderly massaged them, enjoying the smoothness of her skin, the soft warmth of her chest, and the stiffness of her nipples as they bounced between his fingers when he rubbed his hands over them. He alternated this motion with soft squeezes and repeated circumnavigations of her nipples with his fingertips. He knew Tilly loved this and that knowledge put an exclamation point on his pleasure.

As he massaged her, Elmer could feel Tilly's body relax, although, with luck, it would be involuntarily squirming before the day was over. Reaching down, he turned his attention to her belly. Like her breasts, it was now round and soft, unlike its shape when he first noticed its attractive qualities as a high school junior. Fortunately, his standards for a perfect feminine shape had evolved in sync with the somewhat more voluptuous shape Tilly's body now featured. As he pleased her, Elmer reviewed the loveliness of her various body parts one by one, and with each part, he noticed again how he now found them just as beautiful as he had when she, and he, were younger and designed primarily for procreation. Elmer had noticed this phenomena before – that his idea of beauty evolved to match the changes in Tilly's body and he considered, once again, that early in their relationship he had judged Tilly's allure primarily on how cute her body was, whereas now, he found that he not only was still delighted by her physical shape, but also by her sassy way of dealing with the world and the intimacy of their shared history together.

Tilly needed to move briefly to relieve a cramp and used the opportunity to refill their drinks. She leaned against the fireplace and contemplated Elmer's body. He had been skinny when they first got together, but over time, like most men, his midsection had expanded and while he wasn't "fat" he had evolved into a rounder, softer shape just as she had. As she smiled down at Elmer, who was curious about her thoughts, she realized that his current shape was in most ways, superior to the scrawny body he once occupied; even though he had lost some agility, she could now snuggle up against him without fear of being poked by a bony elbow or knee. She sat down on top of him, astride his thighs.

"Here's to Thanksgiving!" she said, clinking their glasses together.

With imaginations assisted by their healthy breakfast, they began a game of taking turns giving thanks for one another's individual body parts, accompanied by special attention to the body part currently being praised. After the major parts had been attended to, they laughingly began giving thanks for more obscure parts or regions. Some of these were not near the surface and required deep massage or shouted praises from close up to communicate with. Both were delighted with the game and, when they ran out of body parts, apart from saving the special ones for last, they began to make up names for imaginary body parts, making the owner of the special part guess where it was. This gave the possessor of the part an opportunity to name whatever part they felt needed more kissing or nibbling, and now and then, the inventor of the part had to try out the proposed location before they could be sure if the guess was correct. This was to be expected when the named parts being given thanks for were the vagilium, the lactoid, the inner buttallius and the like.

After an hour and a half or so, this game was temporarily interrupted by a siren which, after some confusion, was determined to be a smoke alarm. Tilly allowed Elmer to finish tickling her transverse thighristmus and then awkwardly got to her feet and hastened to the kitchen where she found smoke coming from the oven. Two ruined pies resided inside.

Elmer joined her and removed the smoking pies to the snowy back steps. He expected Tilly to be upset about the state of their baking, but instead he found her waiting for him with the bowl of now warm, not at all fluffy, but still delicious whipped cream.

"Let's go give thanks for THIS!" she said.

They returned to the living room and continued giving thanks, now anointing the most ticklish, nipplish, and erogenish body parts with warm, dripping whipped cream, then quickly licking it off to avoid a mess. Sadly, the whipped cream bowl was empty before they wanted it to be, but the thankfulness continued until this giving of thanks reached its climax with protruding parts of their bodies interacting with various concavities belonging to the other. Each body part being given thanks for showed its gratitude for this compliment by reacting with discernable squirming.

Tilly and Elmer concluded the day before Thanksgiving's annual giving of thanks by snuggling together until their breathing had returned to normal. Elmer, delighted and exhausted by his efforts, drifted off into a well-deserved nap, until he heard Tilly's voice, seemingly from far away, "Elmer! Are you ready to wake up and start fucking?"

~~~

12
TILLY'S CHRISTMAS SURPRISE

"Christmas is almost here, Elmer!" Tilly announced.

"How could that be? Halloween was just two days ago, Tilly!"

'Right, and here's my first Christmas catalogue in the mail. It's from 'Luxurious Landfill!' "

Naturally, Tilly found a number of irresistibly cute items as she thumbed through the glossy pages: clever table decorations, tiny flashlights, female sex toys, picnic supplies.

Tilly involuntarily checked her surroundings and turned back to the sex toy page that was casually slipped in between labor saving cleaning contrivances and garden gnomes.

She and Elmer were no strangers to the fun that could be had with what used to be called "marital aids", and it occurred to her that the phallus shaped vibrating device she kept in the drawer of her nightstand was rather old fashioned. To be honest, her trusty toy had seen better days, and even a quick perusal of the items on offer revealed that a lot of innovation and creativity had gone into the design of these devices since she had previously purchased a personal plastic penis.

Tilly was intrigued with the sculptural shapes, soft surfaces, and recharging features of the latest high-tech sex toys. Some were even capable of connecting to the Internet, however, Tilly doubted that she'd want to send anyone an email while she was using a dildo so this feature seemed unnecessary to her. While her old plaything was unambiguously shaped like a protruding part of the male anatomy, these new models looked like soft and colorful Brâncuși sculptures. Tilly closed her eyes for a brief, imaginary road test of the latest styles in these pleasure-producing products and decided it might be time to trade in the old standby for a sportier model featuring a streamlined design and more nimble handling.

She knew Elmer wouldn't object to this acquisition since they often incorporated curious objects into their bedroom frolics and, from time to time, Elmer was even the primary beneficiary of her favorite device. Tilly also knew that buying the item herself would be rather unromantic and might suggest that she intended to save it for use in Elmer's absence. It would be much more romantic and intimate if she could subtly make Elmer think this would make a thoughtful Christmas gift for her. "Let the hints begin," she thought!

Tilly folded the corner of the dildo page down and left the catalogue open on the coffee table.

As was his custom at this time of year, Elmer soon began complaining to Tilly that he had no ideas about what to get her for Christmas.

"Need a hint?" she asked.

"It can't hurt!" he said.

"Well, I do have something in mind. We have an old one, but I hear the new ones are much better."

Elmer looked around. "Is it something we use in the living room?" he asked.

"We certainly could use it in here," Tilly said smiling. Elmer noticed her glance toward the sofa but couldn't remember using any electronic device there. Elmer's usual spot on the sofa had a small dusting of cracker crumbs; could that be a clue?

"How are the new 'whatever-it-ises' different than what we have now?"

"They're much more powerful and colorful! Plus, they're rechargeable and I get so frustrated when the batteries run out when I'm using the old one"

"It sounds like we're talking about a mechanical device?"

"A magical and marvelous mechanical appliance that eases the burdens of women everywhere!" Tilly said, possibly overdramatizing the virtues of her anticipated gift.

"Women everywhere use this device?"

"Lots of women use it whenever they need a little 'pick-me-up'!"

" 'A little pick-me-up' you say!" Elmer said.

He sat down on the sofa and saw the catalogue in which Tilly had turned down the corner of the page. "Hmmm!" he thought, "She doesn't need an electronic garden gnome, even though they are pretty cute!"

"Is this something you'd use every day?" he asked.

"I doubt I'd need to use it every day. And usually you take care of the situation, but you don't always recognize the problem so I have to take care of it myself. Actually, I think you secretly like using this device too and afterwards, everyone feels better."

Elmer wrestled with the problem. What do they use

that needs replacing? Something that would take care of a recurring situation and make everyone feel better when they needed a "pick-me-up?" He looked at the catalogue again and suddenly it was clear what Tilly was getting at!

Elmer was quite proud of his cleverness and took care to wrap Tilly's gift to disguise what it might be. Elmer smiled to himself. "I'll bet she didn't think I'd be able to figure out what she was hinting at!" he thought.

It was their custom on Christmas morning to unwrap their presents to each other together before the rest of the family arrived; some past Christmases had featured rather intimate gifts that neither wanted to have to explain to their children. Elmer unwrapped his gift first and laughed out loud when he found a pair of boxer shorts with a life sized photo of the back of Tilly's head printed on the front. "You always know just what I want, don't you!" he said, giving her a kiss and donning his new underwear.

He handed Tilly her gift. "It's bigger than I expected!" she said.

"I always know just what you want too, my dear!" Elmer said.

Tilly felt a little tingle of anticipation as she opened her present. She unwrapped the paper carefully to prolong the suspense, and, as expected, she was quite surprised. Elmer had gotten her the most colorful and sporty Dust Buster she had ever seen.

"Thank you, Elmer," she said once she recovered her composure. "This IS quite a surprise."

"Well, when you said women used it when they needed a pick-me-up, what else could it have been?"

Making the best of the situation, she playfully applied her device to the front of his new boxer shorts.

"You like what's in my drawers, don't you Tilly?

"Of course I do!" she said.

I think you'll like what's in your drawers too."

Tilly opened the top drawer of the nightstand on her side of the bed and found the most sculptural, colorful, and powerful vibrator she had ever seen, along with an elegant brand of "personal lubricant".

"Oh my god, Elmer!" she said. "This is shocking!"

"What's shocking? That I would buy you a device you might like better than me?" he laughed.

"No, that you understood what I was hinting at! Let's try it out!"

"You know the kids will be here in a couple of hours!" he warned.

"This isn't going to take two hours, Elmer!"

"Elmer reached into the top drawer of his nightstand. Check this out!" he said.

He pressed a button on a small remote control.

"Oh my goodness! You can turn it on from across the room?"

"I can turn it, and you, on from anywhere in the world with a wi-fi connection!"

"I love you, Elmer. And, for the record, you could always turn me on from anywhere even without a wi-fi connection!" ~~~

Tilly and Elmer's Carnal Calendar

ABOUT THE AUTHOR

Gene Clements is an author and artist in Berkeley, California. He has drawn the figure for four decades and his drawings have been exhibited in group shows throughout the Bay Area and at the Seattle Erotic Art Festival. Like Tilly and Elmer, he imagines himself to be eighteen, even though he has not been eighteen for a half century.

Gene grew up in a small town in central Illinois. His mother was an artist and his father an English teacher; no doubt both would be shocked to learn that Gene eventually began to follow in their footsteps, and even more shocked at the content of his efforts. He earned degrees in architecture from the University of Illinois and MIT and practiced architecture and taught architectural history and computer-aided design for many years before turning his focus primarily toward drawing and writing. Gene drew the cover and illustrations for this book on an iPad using the Procreate app.

~~~

Tilly and Elmer's Carnal Calendar

TILLY AND ELMER TITLES

This book and individual story titles in the *Tilly and Elmer's Carnal Calendar* Series, formatted for your favorite e-reader, are also available in the Apple iBook Store, Barnes and Noble Nook Store, Smashwords, Kobo, Sony, the Amazon Kindle Store and other retail outlets.

For more Tilly and Elmer, check out *The Sexy Seniors of South Branch.* In this sweet, nostalgic, funny, and somewhat dirty book, Tilly and Elmer try to recapture their lost youth, leading to some embarrassing and awkward moments. Their experience, imagination, and good humor carry them through though. Most of the time anyway.

Additionally, shocking and scandalous tales of Tilly and Elmer's high school romance can be found in *Coming of Age in South Branch.*

The Sexy Seniors of South Branch and *Coming of Age in South Branch,* are available in paperback, and as individual stories or the complete collection at any e-book retailer. If you're a fan of adult coloring books, many illustrations from these books can be found in print in the *Sexy Seniors* and *Coming of Age* coloring books for grownups.

You can find links to any of these individual titles and collections, as well as more drawings and info, at **TillyandElmer.com**.